G000153780

Trust in your dreams

Hebatt

PRINCE ZAAKI
AND THE
MOMENTOUS BATTLE OF THE KINGDOMS

By Heba Hamzeh

Prince Zaaki and the Momentous Battle of the Kingdoms is published under Emerge, a sectionalized division under Di Angelo Publications, Inc.

Emerge is an imprint of Di Angelo Publications.
Copyright 2021.
Textual copyright Heba Hamzeh in print and digital international dist.
All rights reserved.
Printed in the United States of America.

Di Angelo Publications
4265 San Felipe #1100
Houston, Texas 77027

Library of Congress
Prince Zaaki and the Momentous Battle of the Kingdoms
Limited Edition
ISBN Hardback: 978-1-955690-22-5
ISBN Paperback: 978-1-955690-10-2

Words: Heba Hamzeh
Cover Design: Savina Deianova
Cover Illustration: White Magic Studios
Interior Illustrations: Tamar Volkodav
Interior Design: Kimberly James
Managing Editor: Elizabeth Geeslin Zinn
Editors: Rachel Arbuckle, Ashley Crantas

Downloadable via Kindle, Apple, Nook, and Google Play.

1. Young Adult Fiction --- Fantasy --- Wizards & Witches
2. Young Adult Fiction --- General

Be inspired. Be motivated. Be great.

Dedication:
To my parents for their unconditional love and support
To my three children, my angels, for always inspiring me
to be the best I can be.
To my dear friend, Tommy, for his kindness and believing in me.

Contents

A while ago ... before Prince Zaaki of The Kingdom of Luella's nineteenth birthday

chapter One

I

Once upon a time, on an island hidden off the coast of the Kingdom of Luella, there were two sisters who resided in magnificent temples. There were three temples that stood adjacent to one another, the Temple of Lulu, the Temple of Ella and the Zenith Temple, dominating the Great Courtyard in the City of SADK. The city, perched on the highest point of Pos Island, was ten thousand feet above sea level and shrouded by clouds.

The two sisters, Lulu and Ella, were immortal Goddesses who possessed special powers, one of which was being able to locate children who were born with unique powers. As their powers developed, unable to control their powers, the children were either shunned by their own families or mistreated due to ignorance and fear of the unknown. The Goddesses received visions of a special child in need of their guidance and support when danger crowded the child. They then journeyed afar to rescue the children and bring them to safety within the Zenith Temple. The Zenith Temple housed the century old TransM School, which was run by angels. There, the children were taught how to control their powers and use them wisely.

Goddess Ella, the Goddess of Honesty and Wisdom, wore a gold crown encrusted with blue pearls that matched the colour of her eyes and an ivory toga that flowed over the cloud upon which she floated. Her long golden locks, incessant kindness, eternal youth and remarkable beauty were admired by all around her. Goddess Lulu, the Goddess of Life, wore a golden crown engraved with dazzling ivory pearls and a fitted white toga with a belt of the most brilliant diamonds ever. Her long dark hair matched her piercing boysenberry-coloured eyes. The Goddess of Life was well-known for her infinite love and absolute protection of all living things, as well as her unparalleled radiant beauty and everlasting youth.

Over a hundred years ago, the Goddesses chose Xvisio, the eldest angel, to run the TransM School for them. Xvisio, at three hundred and twenty years of age, had a translucent body and wings with a glistening blue halo magically orbiting his head. He taught many of the angels in the TransM School and thirty years ago had promoted Dowser to deputy head of the school. Dowser, a younger angel at one hundred and seventy-two years of age, possessed a grey body and wings and was eager to become head of the school one day. He would become a translucent angel at the age of two hundred and then would be classed as an elder angel.

To protect the school and students, the Goddesses created

a protective shield encompassing Pos Island. The shield made Pos Island invisible to travelers seeking new land. One could only enter this hidden island by invitation from either of the two Goddesses.

Each morning, the two sisters whispered an ancient phrase in Libnene that caused magical clouds to form beneath their feet to travel on all throughout the temples and surrounding areas. Unlike normal clouds, these satin, white-edged clouds were formed of the purest pink ice crystals with sprinkles of blue-eye magic encompassing them. The blue-eye magic gave added protection to the Goddesses from any evil eyes trying to find and destroy them. Although immortal, the Goddesses could still be harmed, and with every injury they might acquire, their powers would weaken for a few hours or even a few days. The sprinkles of magic helped the Goddesses navigate their personal clouds to wherever they wished to travel. Goddess Ella created a cloud in the shape of a heart whereas Goddess Lulu floated on a cloud shaped like an infinity symbol.

One morning, the two Goddesses floated, seamlessly, on their clouds toward the center of the Hexagonal Courtyard where the Altar of Truth was located. The Altar, submerged in thick, mysterious clouds, was an altar that could see the past, present, has b and future. If someone was taken to the Altar of Truth and did not speak the truth, the Altar would alert the Goddesses and they would deal with the matter accordingly. As the Goddesses visited the Altar daily, they would converse telepathically about the progress of the TransM students and any unrest occurring in the Kingdoms, another of the many gifts bestowed upon them.

"Lulu, we are ready to enroll new students now. Our current students are no longer in need of our assistance and guidance. They are performing very well indeed, and soon, they will graduate to angel level. There are many out there in need of our help," Goddess Ella thought.

Goddess Lulu listened to every word. "My dear sister, I agree. I have had visions of children in danger, who are in hiding because of their uniqueness and differences. Some have been exiled from their own villages and homes because they possess splendid gifts unlike anything the people have seen before. I must find them and bring them here."

"I will prepare for them and notify Xvisio and Dowser to be ready to welcome the new children," Goddess Ella telepathized as she hovered above her glistening pink and white cloud.

"Goddess Ella, The All Wise One has sent me a vision of the chosen one, thus we must prepare for any kind of attack. Only inform Xvisio of this vision presently, as I do not want to worry the others just yet," Goddess Lulu added.

Goddess Ella nodded her head in acknowledgment and then closed her eyes for a moment, sensing an incoming vision. "I have just had a vision of his protector and he will find the chosen one for us. Sister, it is Prince Zaaki Tar of the Kingdom of Luella."

Goddess Lulu gave her a reassuring glance. "Yes, I have just had the same vision. We must return to the school now. I will locate the children and bring them back with me."

They returned to the Zenith Temple. Eight golden pillars stood at the entrance of the Zenith Temple with pale pink columns encircling the temple. These magical columns added a layer of protection to the TransM School, as it was the sacred place where souls would travel through on their way to a new life.

Goddess Lulu and Goddess Ella gracefully floated into Goddess Ella's extravagant room made of gold stone. The clouds beneath their feet gently vanished as they stepped onto the cold stone floor and approached a long marble table in the middle of the grand room. The table, encrusted with pink diamonds that formed an equilateral triangle, had three letters written in each vertex of the triangle, Z, L and E.

Goddess Ella telepathized, "Prince Zaaki will stand with us, Sister, and help protect Pos Island. The All Wise One has bestowed powers onto the Prince, and he will soon be able to summon us and enter The City of SADK without our invitation. Once his powers are awakened and he learns how to use them, he will take his rightful place in the Zenith Temple. It will then become known as the Temple of Zaaki."

Goddess Lulu bowed her head in acknowledgment and

proceeded to transport herself to the location of the first child in need of saving whilst Goddess Ella remained behind to prepare for the new arrival.

Meanwhile, in a dark mystical classroom with light sneaking through the oversized curtains drenched in blue-eye magic sprinkles, Xvisio was teaching a class full of eager students. The amethyst-coloured walls, encrusted with amethyst gems, helped soothe the students from any strain and stress while helping activate their spiritual awareness. The triangular classroom, with an exit door at each vertex, was designed by the Goddesses like every room in the school. In fact, many of the classrooms were triangular in shape with three golden letters, E, L and Z, engraved in each vertex on the ceiling.

Xvisio spread his large angel wings and flew over the students' heads as he delivered the end of his speech. "Each and every eternal soul that comes to you must be given your upmost attention," Xvisio said. "Their journey to reach enlightenment is possible with your guidance, wisdom and patience. I want to congratulate you all on learning to use your powers with control and precision. The knowledge you have gained from the teachings in this school has prepared you for what is about to come. Do not question yourselves, as you are all now ready to take your places in the infinite trans rooms."

All of the students were dressed, according to their

power, in either white, green, red, blue, or yellow cloaks. The student wearing a green cloak specialized in the power of the mind and sun, whereas a student in a red cloak devoted their time to working on the power of the soul and moon. Students wearing yellow cloaks focused on the power of the word and truth. Students in blue cloaks were experts on the power of will and mental power. Only a few very special students wore a white cloak, specializing in the power of realization and fulfillment of the word, as to reach this level required the purest of pure souls.

The students thanked their teacher, banging their fists on the small triangular-shaped marble tables and applauding as they hailed repeatedly, "Angel Xvisio, the greatest angel of all!"

Xvisio wiped a tear from his cheek as he heard their cheers. Trying not to get too emotional, he raised his right hand up in front of his face as his angel wings flapped to keep him in mid-air, and he ordered his students to follow him. He summoned the doors of the classroom open with a sway of his left hand. Some grasped the bottom of their cloaks in their hands and flew after him and others walked quickly behind him as he led them to their places in different TransM rooms.

As he proudly watched his last student enter a TransM room, Xvisio received a message telepathically from Goddess Ella. "Xvisio, please come see me when you are finished with your students."

Xvisio, a powerful angel, could transform into any living creature, so he made his way to Goddess Ella's grand room in the form of a powerful white eagle with a golden yellow beak. There, finding Goddess Ella and Dowser awaiting his prompt arrival, he transformed back into his angel self and bowed down to the Goddess. Xvisio acknowledged his fellow angel with their usual greeting, the opening and closing of his wings, in which Dowser responded likewise.

Goddess Ella looked at Xvisio and explained, "I have called you both here in order to prepare for new students arriving with Goddess Lulu. These students have been hiding their powers and gifts because of the ignorance of people. Therefore, it is imperative that we welcome them, showing them that this school is a safe place for exploring their gifts and gaining insight and knowledge on the purpose of the TransM School."

Dowser interrupted, "I am excited and ready for more students, Goddess Ella. I am keen to meet them and start their training."

Xvisio agreed with a silent bow of his head.

Goddess Ella acknowledged Dowser's enthusiasm and reiterated, "Please make sure the students are comfortable with us and reinforce that they are safe here under our protection. Xvisio and Dowser, you will each be receiving 50 new students and Goddess Lulu will be transmitting their details to you."

Dowser replied, "Yes, yes, of course. I will await Goddess Lulu's messages."

"Very good. That is all. Dowser, please go and make the

necessary arrangements." Goddess Ella dismissed Dowser.

"Goddess Ella, I will go and prepare for them at once," Dowser exclaimed as he respectfully bowed down to the Goddess and flew out of her room.

Goddess Ella watched Dowser leave and then turned to Xvisio. "Xvisio, now that we are alone, I must inform you of one of the students. Goddess Lulu and I have had visions of a boy who will come to us in an unusual way. The All Wise One has chosen him personally, and when you meet him, you will see why. The world is changing, and while good is spreading, evil is even more so. The world balance is no longer equal, and his path will be to restore the balance of good. He will face many challenges, and there will come a time when he will have to prove himself worthy of this role, hence Goddess Lulu and myself have accepted responsibility to watch over and guide him. In due course, when he does honour us with his presence, you will show him the TransM rooms."

"Of course, Goddess Ella. The All Wise One has chosen him, which means only one thing." Xvisio trembled as he spoke.

"Yes, as foreseen by The All Wise One, we are nearing the time of the Harb World War where evil attempts to take over the world. Pos Island is at risk of being exposed. If this happens, Shaytan will take control of the TransM rooms; it will cause mayhem and disorder amongst all the souls," Goddess Ella calmly proclaimed, trying to hide her fear.

Xvisio replied, "I have faith in The All Wise One and

know that good will prevail in the end. Let us hope that he can successfully defeat evil and restore the balance of good in the world. As always, I am completely at your disposal. Anything I can do to help this chosen one, I will."

Xvisio respectfully bowed down to the Goddess as he walked backwards, departing her room.

chapter Two

II

The soft echo of swords clashing swept through the long entwining halls of the Royal Palace as two disguised men fenced violently in the Royal Garden under the scorching red sun. One man, wearing a white mask over his face, advanced deftly forward. The other, a black mask cloaking his appearance, retreated back.

The mysterious, white-masked stranger cornered his opponent on the grand staircase leading to the back entrance of the palace. His illuminating silver button-pointed sabre poked his assailant in his chest, causing him to lose balance and loosen his clasp on the Luellan grip handle. The defenseless masked man, trying to reach his lightweight sabre, was sweating profusely as he redirected all his energy into stretching his right arm towards his weapon.

"Surrender, my good friend! You will never be able to

defend yourself against me," the white-masked person advised while simultaneously pushing his opponent into the edge of the olive-green marble staircase.

"Never!"

Suddenly, the black-masked man grabbed his sabre and advanced for attack. After slashing their weapons at each other for another hour and a half, they both halted for a few seconds to catch their breath before resuming the fencing stance, with one hand raised in the air above their heads. Both men in combat possessed a scientific art in fencing which was breathtaking to watch. In one corner of the purple-grassed garden, the animals were grazing while still being fixated on the bout.

"Begin," shouted one of the men.

Recommencing, they fenced brilliantly, attacking and defending well until sunset, when the white-masked stranger realised he must end this fight without further delay. Aware that his meeting had already begun, he initiated the face-off.

The two unrecognisable combatants stood face to face holding their swords at each other and began to circle them one hundred and eighty degrees in alternate directions. Suddenly, without hesitation the white-masked opponent cleverly triple somersaulted over his challenger and, taking him by surprise, tripped him up from behind and stood over his vulnerable body.

During this precise moment in time, whilst they were cautiously staring at each other, absolute lull filled the palace gardens. It was as if, just for that second, the animals stopped breathing in anticipation of the next move.

Thereupon the white-masked stranger dropped his sword, placing out his hand to help the black-masked man rise to his feet. Instantaneously they both removed their headgear, revealing their identity. Protectius was unusually tall and extremely muscular with dark hair and handsome features. He laughed as he wiped away the sweat running down his forehead. Both Protectius and Prince Zaaki were skilled and gifted swordsmen who enjoyed a competitive yet peaceful sword duel on occasion.

"Good fight, Prince Zaaki," Protectius panted in his strong Magnetian accent as he put his powerfully built arm around the Prince's shoulder.

Prince Zaaki chuckled, "Not too bad yourself."

As they began to walk towards the stairs of the Palace, Protectius glared up at the fading light in the sky. He knew full well that they were late for an important meeting regarding the big event that was taking place very soon in the Kingdom.

"We must hurry, your parents will be waiting. Meet you in fifteen minutes in the conference room," said Protectius as he approached his hoverboard and flew away.

Prince Zaaki stood for a minute, gazing at his garden and all the colourful, exotic animals going about their lives. He silently thanked the Goddesses and his parents for his truly blessed life and exited the garden by foot, whilst his servile hoverboard hovered by his side.

chapter Three
III

Within the Royal Palace of the Kingdom of Luella, a gentle ballad filled the Royal Conference Room. The gold hardwood floor sparkled under the lights, and the walls, clothed with gold and emerald paper, matched the extravagant emerald chandeliers. King Zok invited his guests to sit at the large table, which was comprised of white and silver marble laced with gold, placed in the center of the room. The Royals sat on gold throne chairs, which had intricately carved detailing and emerald green fabric.

King Salam and Queen Hadia, the King and Queen of Yistyyim were King Zok's honoured guests. The Kingdom of Yistyyim, situated north of the Kingdom of Luella, was twice as big as the Kingdom of Luella. The King of Yistyyim personally trained his army to keep the peace, as he was an advocate of peace and harmony, thus King Zok requested his help during the Battle of the Kingdoms.

King Zok, a tall and well-built monarch, wore a long olive-green tunic embellished with gold thread across his broad shoulders. On top of his tunic, he wore a black and gold surcoat depicting the emblem of his family, the Tars. The emblem was the Royal Stone of Luelza, the majestic and mystic great black pyramid, which was located on the top of the Great Snow Blue Mountain. A magnificent gold crown, encrusted with green diamonds, sat regally on his head. Around his neck lay a heavy 24 carat gold chain, with an olive-green diamond pendant in the shape of the Royal Sword of Luella. King Zok carried a long golden scepter with an extravagant pink crystal as the centerpiece at the top, symbolizing his power and strength. The pink crystal was a gift from Zaeem, head of the Magnetians, who had taken it from the powerful pink crystal rocks in Magnetia. King Zok exuded royal authority and sovereignty in his attire and attitude.

King Salam, a short and stumpy monarch, wore a taupe-coloured tunic with gold-thread and a light blue surcoat that depicted the emblem of his family. He wore a smaller crown to that of King Zok, also made of the finest gold and encrusted with very rare blue diamonds. His peaceful and regal demeanor resonated throughout the Royal Conference Room.

Both Queen Tee-Tee and Queen Hadia wore silk pastel-coloured gowns laced in expensive trimmings and feminine petit gold crowns encrusted with diamonds. Both Queens embellished their royal attire with gold and pearl jewellery.

The Royal Conference Room was filled with the most extravagant decorations, from exotic flowers in one-metre-tall golden vases to embroidered famous paintings hung on the walls framed in the finest solid gold. The room was perfectly fit for all the Royalty present and contained an air of supremacy and eminence.

King Zok stomped his scepter on the ground and opened the meeting.

"The Battle of the Kingdoms is upon us once again as new land has been found and will be the prize for this monumental competition. I have spoken to the head judge, and he has secured the co-ordinates of the new land until the award ceremony takes place. I appreciate you, King Salam, travelling to our Kingdom to discuss your part in this battle. Queen Tee-Tee and I hope your stay with us at the Royal Palace will be pleasant. Anything you require please let one of the staff know and they will try to meet your demands as best they can. I would also like to offer my gratitude for your support during this event. Know that when the time comes for your Kingdom to hold this event, I will reciprocate."

King Zok surrounded himself with five of his best advisors, whilst the King of Yistyyim was accompanied by three of his own. The advisors listened and recommended ideas for the future major event, all the while drawing up contracts for the discussions taking place.

Queen Tee-Tee scanned the room for her son to no avail, hence she summoned one of the guards standing by.

The guard leant down his ear to the Queen as she murmured, "Where is he? Why is he always late? Someone go and find out where my son is and tell him to hurry. Quickly, before the King notices that his successor is not by his side."

Queen Tee-Tee scanned the room once more to find Protectius missing as well before whispering to the guard, "And where is Protectius? The King needs his Army General as well. Look in the grounds for them, both. I have a feeling they are still fencing. What disarray!"

'When will they learn that they must always be here to welcome our guests,' Queen Tee-Tee angrily thought to herself, trying her best to stay calm and composed. She did not want her guests to feel uncomfortable in the slightest.

Some of the Queen's guards began to disperse as Star, sylphlike as always, dashed to the Queen's side.

"Your Majesty, the Prince will be here shortly. He lost track of time whilst fencing with Protectius," Star whispered in the Queen's ear.

Queen Hadia placed her hand on Queen Tee-Tee's shoulder reassuringly. Queen Hadia had a son the same age as Prince Zaaki, so she knew exactly what the Queen of Luella felt addressing her guests without her son.

"Let us discuss the security issue of the games now. Can you asseverate that your army will keep the peace at every cost, King Salam?" the King of Luella asked, and before giving his guests an opportunity to respond, he followed, "Of course, my army general Protectius and his army will work with you closely to maintain a peaceful atmosphere amongst all the audience members. Where is Protectius?" King Zok paused to scan the room. "Come to think of it, where is my son?"

As soon as the King summoned the guards to search for the Prince and Protectius, they nonchalantly walked in.

"Good evening, father." Prince Zaaki bowed to his father after which he gave his mother a kiss on the cheek.

"Your Highness," Protectius bowed in front of the King and Queen of Luella then preceded to bow in front of the King and Queen of Yistyyim.

Prince Zaaki and Star shared a few stolen glances whilst the introductions were taking place, until an extremely dashing young man walked through the doors of the grand ballroom and captured Star's attention. The women in the room were reduced to silence as they felt the overwhelming presence of this remarkably well-dressed handsome man. Prince Zaaki and Protectius, unphased by the latest arrival, continued to chatter amongst themselves.

Upon seeing his son, Prince Yalem, enter the room, King Salam stood up and walked towards him.

Prince Yalem was tall and debonair, with dark hair, dark brown eyes and an olive complexion. He wore a fitted taupe jacket with gold thread and gold buttons over tailored black trousers and a fancy black shirt.

"Oh good, you are here," said the King of Yistyyim, clapping his hand onto his son's shoulder as he continued. "This is my son, Prince Yalem the Third."

Prince Zaaki was the first of his family to shake Prince Yalem's hand, and thus took it upon himself to introduce the young man to his parents and the royal advisors. He led Prince Yalem and King Yistyyim to the table, and after the formalities, they took their respective seats. The kings and the queens sat in pairs, and Prince Zaaki sat beside his father. He immediately joined in a lively discussion with Protectius and the King of Yistyyim on security matters for the royal guests, contestants, judges and spectators of the events.

Prince Zaaki was blissfully unaware of how Prince Yalem took one glimpse at Star and, struck by her beauty, subtly moved himself to be closer to her. While Yalem rivaled for Star's affections, Protectius offered a third of his army for the event, and the King of Yistyyim seconded his support of peace.

"I will offer half of my army," the King of Yistyyim said, "but I need something in return. You have an unlimited supply of energy in your land, and the Kingdom of Yistyyim is in desperate need of a continuous and reliable energy supply line. If you agree to supply my Kingdom with part of your surplus energy, I can send for my engineers and builders. They will create and build an underground transporting mechanism from your Kingdom to mine, thus giving us some of your energy supply in these desperate times. You will be in control of the amount sent to my Kingdom at all times, and I will regularly consult with you on the quantity needed."

Prince Zaaki quietly conferred with his father and his advisors.

"I will oblige the requisite you ask for, on one condition," King Zok announced to King Salam. "My men and your men will work together to build this transport mechanism in a combined effort to supply your land with energy. We are always happy to help our fellow neighbours."

After much deliberation, the plans for this momentous event were set into motion. Protectius was given the hardest task; to keep the peace in order to prevent riots and fights from occurring in the lead-up to and duration of the games, with the help of both armies. Prince Zaaki suggested to King Zok that he wanted to head the project for the construction of the energy transportation, thus the King of Yistyyim interrupted and insisted that both Prince Zaaki and Prince Yalem will liaise to oversee this project successfully, together.

"I am assured that this project will be a great success under the supervision and guidance of Prince Zaaki and Prince Yalem. King Salam, I trust you and your Kingdom, as you have shown nothing but kindness and support to my Kingdom for many years. Yalem, you will stay with us at the Palace until this operation is completed. Zaaki, I am sure that you and Yalem will build a great friendship as well as structure an energy supply route into the Kingdom of Yistyyim. Now that everything is settled, I am content. King Salam, do you agree?" King Zok rhetorically questioned.

"The dialogue between both our Kingdoms today has comforted and pleased me greatly. I am enamored at your hospitality, King Zok and Queen Tee-Tee, and I would like to express my gratitude. In return, I can promise you that the games taking place in your Kingdom forthwith will run smoothly and without any problems. I will personally work with Protectius for the last few days of my visit to show him some useful tactics and methods, which produce sustainable peace. Protectius, you will marshal this whole event, enforcing the law in a way that will gain respect from all attending the battle. Many spectators are travelling from distant Kingdoms to watch this glorious spectacle."

"Let us all now retire for a well-deserved rest before dinner. The King and I invite you all to a dinner amongst the stars," Queen Tee-Tee hesitated as she saw Prince Yalem subtly flirting with Star.

Queen Tee-Tee cleared her throat.

"All will be revealed tonight. Now, there will be two helpers waiting in your suites to tend to your needs and one masseur in each suite to offer you an ancient Luellan massage that will leave you feeling revitalized and ready for this evening's dinner."

The King and Queen of Yistyyim were escorted to their Royal Suite by three well-built seven-foot guards.

"Star, it has been an honour to make your acquaintance. I hope we can continue our talk this evening?" Prince Yalem knelt down before her as he took her hand and kissed it.

Star graciously smiled so as not offend the guests of the

King and Queen of Luella. Prince Yalem took her sweet silence as acceptance and departed to his quarters.

Prince Zaaki and King Zok finished signing some documents with King Zok's advisors and began to walk out of the Royal Conference Room when Prince Zaaki noticed Star standing motionless, staring into thin air.

"Are you coming, Star?"

"Sorry Prince—I mean Your Highness—sorry, I mean Zaaki. Yes, I am, I am right behind you." Star fumbled with her words and rushed towards the exit as she saw Queen Tee-Tee depart.

Prince Zaaki stopped Star. "Is everything alright with you? You seem distracted."

Star stared into Prince Zaaki's eyes, knowing that her love for him was beyond anything she could have ever imagined. She felt torn between whether or not she should inform him that Prince Yalem was flirting with her, because she knew where her heart lay, and it was for only one prince—Prince Zaaki.

"No, not at all. I must go and help Her Majesty get ready for tonight," Star insisted and gave Prince Zaaki a reassuring smile and a kiss on his cheek before hurrying to Queen Tee-Tee's side.

chapter Four
IV

Queen Tee-Tee planned a small private dinner party under the diamond-like stars in the Royal Ballroom. Once all the guests were seated at the elongated glass dining table, the Queen pointed up, and forthwith, the high ceilings of the ballroom split down the middle and pulled apart, opening to the glittering night sky. The guests all had front row seats to this spectacular view from the comfort of the royal dining armchairs. The dazzling platinum-gold full moon was the centerpiece amongst the gleaming bright stars that filled the night sky.

"Queen Tee-Tee, you will never fail to astound and impress me. This is the perfect way to end our successful meeting with the King of Yistyyim. I now order everyone to enjoy this miraculous evening, for tomorrow will be the start of the real hard work preparing for the games," King Zok cheerfully demanded, completely mesmerized by the beautiful display in the transformed

Royal Ballroom.

"Did you also have something to do with the perfect alignment of the stars tonight?" joked the King of Yistyyim.

The guests all broke into laughter, which allowed everyone to relax and enjoy the evening for what it was: a spectacularly entertaining and intimate evening of the royalty of the Kingdom of Luella and the Kingdom of Yistyyim.

"Actually, I asked a favour from the Goddesses, and it seems to have worked," Queen Tee-Tee replied sarcastically.

The King and Queen of Yistyyim looked again at the stars and realised that the stars were aligned to spell out 'Shoukran Lal Malak Ou Malakeh Yistyyim,' which means in the Libnene dialect, Thank you to the King and Queen of Yistyyim. Shooting stars crossed over the writing, giving the impression of fireworks blazing out from every letter.

"Prince Yalem, tell me about your Kingdom. Do you have a community that resides in the sea similar to our Luellan Sizzlites?"

"Yes, we most certainly do." Prince Yalem cleared his throat and resumed, "We have the Sizzlites of Yistyyim. They are our sea protectors." Prince Yalem gave a short, non-informative answer as he was far more interested in charming the beautiful Star.

"Now, my dear, dear guests, I have another small surprise. Please hold onto your chairs and stay seated. We are about to take off," Queen Tee-Tee announced as she gave a wave of her hand to one of her servants.

The dining table and chairs began to levitate, and guests gasped with excitement as they gripped their seats tightly. The chairs, along with their delighted passengers, slowly rose up into the air as if they were closing in on the stars. The sounds of the nocturnal animals could be clearly heard alongside the music played by the Luellan orchestra.

They halted at the open ceiling of the ballroom, and the servants, dressed in purple attire, served the guests on their purple and silver hoverboards.

The corners of the ballroom were covered in a foggy white smoke that began to clear, and levitated, white satin couches appeared. The stunned guests were muted by the visuals of the whole evening. Forthwith the night progressed as if in slow motion, with all the guests laughing, eating and enjoying one another's company. Prince Yalem continued to beguile Star with his suave charm throughout the course of the evening. Although his debonair character was hard to resist, Star was far more interested in peering over at Prince Zaaki, who was deep in conversation with his father and the King of Yistyyim.

Protectius stood silently by Queen Tee-Tee's side, watching the guests dance amongst the heavenly white clouds that circled their feet. Queen Tee-Tee's caring nature, which could also be mistaken for curiosity and a prying eye, led her to watch Prince Yalem carefully as she was aware of his interest with Star. The Queen decided to stroll towards Prince Yalem. Protectius followed her, knowing full well of her intentions. '

"Yalem, tell me about yourself. What do you do when you are not accompanying your father on expeditions?" Queen Tee-Tee enquired.

"Star, are you enjoying the dinner? I have never tasted such delicious food," Protectius questioned Star, hoping to refrain Prince Yalem's attempt to sweep Star off her feet and away from Prince Zaaki's love for her.

"What's wrong, Protectius? Why are you so interested in the food all of a sudden?" Star curiously stared at Protectius before answering his unusual question. "If you really must know, I found the purple grass and bark soup to be sensational, but the lionfish wings were slightly undercooked for my liking. And the "

Whilst Star described each plate with great passion, Protectius tried to feign interest, making dogged efforts to camouflage his yawns.

After a memorable evening, which ended with all the guests residing on floating balconies, gazing at the wondrous night sky, Prince Zaaki was still deep in conversation with King Zok. When he glimpsed Star and Prince Yalem alone on a balcony, the Prince abruptly requested dismissal from his father and flew on his hoverboard to Star.

"Star. Prince Yalem." Prince Zaaki held Star's hand to his

lips and softly placed a kiss.

Prince Yalem started a meaningless conversation with Prince Zaaki, but Prince Zaaki was uninterested. Not listening to a word Prince Yalem was speaking, he softly pulled Star close to his torso.

"Star, may I have a quiet word with you?"

"I have some things to tend to, thus I will leave. Star, it was a pleasure. Prince Zaaki," Prince Yalem said as he bowed down to Star and Prince Zaaki and left the balcony.

There was an uncomfortable silence between them for a moment, which made Prince Zaaki feel the need to say something—anything—to break the quietude and let Star know how he felt. He leaned in and whispered in her ear, "I have missed you, my beautiful Star. I am sorry, my love, for I have been preoccupied with preparations for the Battle of the Kingdoms."

Star took a step back from the prince, scanning the depths of his piercing blue eyes. She felt his words so deeply and she thought of all the things she truly wanted to tell him, but she chose her words dutifully.

"I understand, Your Highness, the Queen has also asked me to tend to our guests from Yistyyim and meet all their needs," she replied, trying to hide her sadness.

Prince Zaaki could see in Star's eyes that she missed him and only said what she thought he wanted to hear.

Politely responding to Star's busy schedule, Prince Zaaki said, "I hope the Yistyyim's are not causing you problems. Prince Yalem seems quite extravagant."

"He does come across as quite extravagant at first, but I can assure you that he is not. Actually, he is quite nice once you get to know him."

"That's good to know, as I will be working with him in the coming weeks." Prince Zaaki held Star's hand and continued, "Star, I watch you with my mother and how you take care of her. Your kindness and good heart shines through. Every time I pass you in the Palace, I am brought to my knees by your elegance and beauty. I have come to realize that I only want you by my side. I want to spend all my life making you happy. I have fallen completely in love with you."

Star mesmerised in Prince Zaaki's presence and completely lost in his words, gazed passionately into his eyes, wonderfully speechless.

"Your eyes tell me you feel the same, my love," Prince Zaaki said as he was captivated by her gaze.

After a few moments of lovingly admiring each other, Star
spoke, "And I, too, am in love with you, my Prince—I mean, Zaaki. I have been since I first laid eyes upon you. In all honesty, I have but one reservation, and it haunts me. I must tell you so that we can move past it."

"Without question, I want you to feel comfortable enough to always tell me when something bothers or upsets you. Tell me what this matter is, and we shall resolve it together, posthaste," Prince Zaaki comforted Star.

"Prince Zaaki come quickly! You are needed!" Protectius called out, fast approaching them on a hoverboard.

The Prince, still holding Star's hand, looked into her eyes, not wanting to leave her side, but she reluctantly gave him an approving nod to go.

And with this, his hand slipped away from hers. She removed something from her pocket, placed this small object in his hand and whispered in his ear, "Keep this close to you until you return to me."

Prince Zaaki glanced in his hand and saw a silver metal compass engraved with the words, 'My Dearest Zaaki, always find your way back to me. Love forever, Star.' He placed the compass close to his heart, inside the chest pocket of his jacket, affectionately kissed Star, and departed.

chapter Five

V

Protectius whispered in Prince Zaaki's ear some urgent news, and Prince Zaaki hastily left the party unnoticed, making his way to Strongheart, his magical purple and silver flying horse, in the Royal Stables of the palace. Without any time to waste, Strongheart flew Prince Zaaki towards Pos Island where the Goddesses anxiously awaited his arrival.

When they reached the mountains of Luella, Strongheart flew at a higher altitude to fly directly over the Great Snow Blue Mountain.
They reached the other side of this magnificent mountain, and Strongheart began to descend as they approached flatter land.

Prince Zaaki looked at the ground below and noticed smoke coming from a house. He ordered Strongheart to land in a clearing near this house, looked at the watch on his wrist, and pressed a button that turned on VS. He asked his VS what his current location was.

VS responded, "You are in Ardmiya, Prince Zaaki."

Prince Zaaki quickly dismounted and rushed to see if anyone was inside the house ablaze with fire. He recklessly barged in, not fearing for his own life. He had only one thing in his mind; to help whoever was inside. He heard screaming coming from one of the bedrooms and hurriedly made his way to the door, skillfully avoiding the furious flames. Prince Zaaki tried a few times to push the bedroom door open with the force of his shoulder, but the door remained firmly shut.

Strongheart appeared, and with one powerful kick, pulled the door from its hinges, shooting it across the bedroom where it crashed into the wardrobe. Prince Zaaki searched the room to find a little boy and girl hiding under the bed, crying and riddled with fear.

"Come with me quickly," Prince Zaaki urged as he reached his hand under the bed, lifted the boy with one hand and placed him on Strongheart's back.

Prince Zaaki held the girl's hand and shielded her from the flames as they exited the house. Briskly, Strongheart flew the boy out of the house and to safety, far from the blazing fire. The house exploded into a furnace, throwing Prince Zaaki and the girl a few meters through the air, where they landed in a cloud of ash on the muddy ground.

Prince Zaaki slowly lifted himself up and peered over at the girl lying on her front, motionless by his side.

He checked to see if she was breathing and then, without hesitation, carried the unconscious girl towards Strongheart and the boy.

As Prince Zaaki lay the girl down next to Strongheart, the little boy jumped off the horse's back, knelt by her side and began to cry out, "Ivory, wake up! Please, please, Ivory!"

The little girl started to cough, and Prince Zaaki helped her raise her head and slowly sit up.

"What is your name?" Prince Zaaki asked the boy.

"I am Immanuel, and this is my sister, Ivory," he replied, wiping his tears away as he hugged his sister.

"I'm ok, Immanuel. I'm ok, don't worry, I promised you, I will never leave you," muttered Ivory, coughing out the fumes she had inhaled.

"Ivory and Immanuel, I am Prince Zaaki, and this is my horse, Strongheart. Ivory, where are your parents?" Prince Zaaki asked.

Ivory looked at Immanuel before she hesitantly spoke, "Our parents and sister, Karena, disappeared twelve months ago or thereabout, and I have been looking after Immanuel. We have tried to search for them, but we cannot go too far by foot, as Immanuel tires quickly. I promised him that we will never stop searching for them. We miss Karena and my father and mother terribly and we want them to come home."

"How old are you, Ivory?" Prince Zaaki asked.

"I am twelve, and my brother is ten years old. My sister Karena is fourteen now," responded Ivory, sobbing and holding her brother's hand tightly.

"I just have one more question if that's ok?" Prince Zaaki calmly asked.

As Ivory nodded, her russet-coloured curls fell across her ash-stained face in disarray. She swiped the hair away from her unusual and rare eyes, big and white with a hint of blue in them. Shaken and distressed, she began to wipe the ash residue from her cheeks and button nose with the aid of the ripped dress she wore. The colour of the dress was unclear as it was covered in soot.

"How did the fire in your home start?" Prince Zaaki questioned.

Ivory's little voice trembled with fear as she answered, "I was washing and peeling potatoes for tomorrow's breakfast, after putting Immanuel to bed, when I heard glass shatter in the living room. When I ran to see what it was, I just saw a fire starting in the middle of the living room, so I rushed to Immanuel and woke him up."

Tears rolled down Ivory's cheeks as she recalled the horrific incident. She tried to wipe her tears with her hands, but she smudged the soot deeper into her skin.

She took a deep breath and carried on. "We tried to walk out of his bedroom, but the fire spread so quickly, and the flames were too strong. So I made a decision to go back into the bedroom, close the door and place a blanket at the foot of the door to try to stop the fumes and fire from entering. After that, Immanuel and I hid under the bed. Then we heard your voice."

Ivory looked up at Prince Zaaki and stopped trembling.

In a slighter calmer tone, Ivory said, "You saved us. Thank you, Prince Zaaki. I am forever grateful."

"Thank you for being so strong and brave, Ivory, and for telling me all of this. You saved your brother's life and your own. Strongheart and I will take care of you. We have a special place where you will be safe until we find your parents and sister. You have to trust us and come with us now, before whoever tried to burn your home returns." Prince Zaaki requested, holding out his hand hoping that they would trust him and grab his hand.

Immanuel was a frail little boy with loose fitting, homemade clothes, now covered in soot, and over-grown curly dark brown hair. Ivory noticed her brother shaking like a leaf and placed her arm around him comfortingly.

Immanuel leaned into Ivory's ear and whispered something.

Then they both ran into Prince Zaaki's arms and gave him a tight hug.

They were all on Strongheart's back in mid-air, flying to Pos Island when Prince Zaaki inquired, "Do you know anyone who disliked your parents or wanted to hurt them? Or any reason for them to disappear?"

Both the children were silent and bowed their heads, reluctant to answer the questions.

"If I am to find your parents and reunite you all, I will need to know everything. Please do not be frightened. Whatever it is, I will help you both. I promise."

After a few moments of silence, Ivory accepted Prince Zaaki's offer to find her missing family members. She explained to Prince Zaaki that her family was different. Her father, Callum, had a gift of seeing into the future. Her mother, Panacea, could heal people with her hands and sometimes used a magic potion she made from the water in the river in Ardmiya found below ground. Ivory expressed how much her parents tried to hide their gifts from everyone, but to their detriment, they selflessly used their gifts to help people who needed healing. This led to their secret falling into the wrong hands. Ivory continued to explain how she believed that they were kidnapped for their gifts. She elucidated further and Prince Zaaki began to understand why they disappeared and exactly who could help trace them.

Strongheart informed the Prince that they were arriving at Pos Island.

Goddess Lulu and Goddess Ella, aware of Prince Zaaki's imminent arrival, floated on their clouds by the grand entrance of the Zenith Temple to greet him. Goddess Ella swayed her left hand from left to right and magically opened the colossal doors.

Strongheart flew through the entrance and straight past the Goddesses, landing five metres from them. Prince

Zaaki dismounted Strongheart, helping the children off as well. Immanuel, nervous and apprehensive, hid behind Prince Zaaki and tugged on his trouser leg. In contrast, the fearless Ivory walked boldly up to the Goddesses and put her hand out to shake their hands. When the Goddesses just smiled, Ivory was confused and slightly embarrassed, but that turned to relief when Goddess Lulu finally approached her and gave her a warm embrace.

"It is so nice to finally meet you, Ivory. We have been waiting for you and your family," Goddess Lulu mentioned as she gave Ivory a warm hug.

"And this little man, behind Prince Zaaki, must be Immanuel," Goddess Ella voiced as she held out her hand towards Immanuel.

Immanuel slowly let go of Prince Zaaki and showed his face. Then, after gazing over at his sister standing by Goddess Lulu, he took Goddess Ella's hand and she led him down the hall of the Zenith Temple. Everyone followed and Immanuel began to retell the story to the Goddesses.

Finally, Ivory and Immanuel felt safe in the presence of the almighty Goddesses and relieved that Prince Zaaki promised to find their parents and sister. After hearing their story, the Goddesses looked at each other and received a vision of the past of Karena living with Ivory and Immanuel. Forthwith they telepathically summoned Karena, a current student of the TransM School.

Goddess Ella whispered to Immanuel, "We have good news for you regarding Karena," and before Goddess

Ella could finish her sentence, Karena came running up to Immanuel and Ivory. She embraced them both tightly, tears of relief running down all of their faces.

Karena was well-dressed in a school uniform, covered by a blue cloak with her golden angel wings protruding through. She had long, straight brown hair braided neatly, and her angelic beauty was on full display.

"You are excused from your classes today, Karena, and you may show your sister and brother around the school," Goddess Lulu instructed Karena with a warm smile.

"Karena, I will organize two additional beds to be placed in your bedroom. I am sure Immanuel and Ivory would very much like to be close to you after their ordeal," Goddess Ella informed Karena.

Prince Zaaki explained to the children that they would attend this special school and learn to use their gifts for good and to help others. As the Prince bid the children farewell, he promised that he would find their parents and safely bring them to the TransM School.

Karena walked off, hand in hand with Ivory and Immanuel, to show them around the TransM School. The Goddesses led Strongheart and Prince Zaaki to the conference room to privately discuss how to keep Baal and Karena's powerful gifts under control.

Goddess Lulu explained to Prince Zaaki that Karena's capabilities were intensifying, and with just one touch of any person, she could see their past, present and future.

Prince Zaaki, unaware that Baal was hiding behind a pillar in the conference room listening intently to the conversation, continued to explain that he would return to the place he found Ivory and Immanuel and search for clues to help him find their parents.

Baal, a thirteen-year-old boy with an electric silver-white glow circling his body, stood nervously trying to hold his breath so as to go unnoticed. He had short black hair and wore a white TransM cloak, blissfully unaware of the reason behind the colour coding of the cloaks.

Whilst the Goddesses were informing Prince Zaaki of their knowledge regarding Panacea and Callum, Strongheart noticed a white cloak sneaking out from behind a pillar. He started trotting towards Baal, who, seeing Strongheart heading towards him, knew he had been found.

"I'm sorry. I overheard your conversation, Prince Zaaki," Baal apologized as he stepped forward from behind the pillar.

"Baal, what are you doing here? Shouldn't you be in a class?" Prince Zaaki asked.

With a guilty look on his face, Baal glanced at Goddess Lulu and stayed silent.

"Baal, we will talk about this later, but now you must go finish your classes for the day. Before dinner, please come see me," Goddess Lulu said sternly.

"Yes, Goddess Lulu, I will. And my apologies again for

listening in on your private conversation, but I think I can help. I want to help Prince Zaaki find Karena's parents. Please, please, I want to help," Baal begged as he stared at Goddess Lulu.

Goddess Lulu replied, "Baal, we appreciate that you want to help, and it shows to us that you are a kind and caring soul. Sadly, where Prince Zaaki is going is not safe for you. Right now, I need you to focus on taking control of your gift and learning more about the TransM School. I promise when you are ready, your time will come to help others, but first you must go back to your lessons."

Goddess Ella interrupted and said, "Come with me Baal. I will take you back to your class."

Baal, disheartened, looked down at the ground and reluctantly followed Goddess Ella out of the room. "Baal," Prince Zaaki loudly spoke, "thank you for wanting to help. You are exceedingly kind, and I will never forget the courage and compassion you showed today. Please listen to the Goddesses, as they have your best interest at heart. By attending all your lessons, you will be ready sooner than you think in assisting me help others in the Kingdom of Luella. I will be back soon, and you can show me your powers that I've heard so much about and tell me all about what your lessons."

Baal nodded as he reluctantly departed, still upset that he was not allowed to help find Karena's parents.

chapter Six
VI

As the sun awoke and crept up behind the Zenith Temple, it filled the sky with tunnels of light penetrating through the clouds. With sunrays pouring onto Pos Island, warming up the day and shining down on the magical land, Prince Zaaki mounted Strongheart and gazed up at the sky.

"Strongheart, what an extraordinary yet so ordinary sunrise. The land, the grass, the trees and the flowers are all aglow with the rays of this wondrous beauty in the sky above. It fills my heart with joy to see such a stunning awakening to the new day. I have a good feeling that we will find Ivory's parents," Prince Zaaki softly spoke as he breathed it all in.

Strongheart spread his wings and began to gallop. Prince Zaaki held onto Strongheart's reigns tightly as he took off into the sky and flew them away from the City of SADK. Strongheart soared over the Zenith Temple and headed towards Ardmiya in the Kingdom of Luella.

"Prince Zaaki, you have an incoming call from the Palace," VS alerted.

"Put me through, VS," Prince Zaaki replied as he lifted his wrist up to his eyeline.

King Zok appeared on his VS and said, "My son, I need your presence at the Palace posthaste. The King and Queen of Yistyyim are making their way back to their Kingdom, and Prince Yalem is remaining with us. He is awaiting your return to commence work on the energy supply line."

"Yes, of course, Father. I will be with you very soon. I have one thing I must tend to and will make my way back to the palace."

Strongheart began to lower his altitude as he approached Ardmiya, and Prince Zaaki scanned the ground below. They searched for signs of Karena's parents and for clues pertaining to their disappearance in the land of Ardmiya but to no avail.

"Strongheart, whoever kidnapped or took Karena's parents is not holding them in Ardmiya. We must expand our search and not allow any more time to pass. I will need to call on the sword's help."

Prince Zaaki drew his sword from its scabbard hung on his waist and held it in front of him, facing up towards the sky. "I call on the power of my sword to help me find Callum and Panacea, the mother and father of Karena,

Immanuel and Ivory."

With those words, the sword began to glow a blinding purple light. Prince Zaaki proceeded to tilt the sword ninety degrees facing forward, and a path of purple light appeared, leading the way to Callum and Panacea.

"Follow this light, Strongheart," Prince Zaaki ordered as he patted the horse on his back.

Strongheart, without any hesitation, followed the magical purple path as it led them up the Great Snow Blue Mountain. Suddenly, nearing the top of the mountain, Strongheart slowed down and came to a near halt as the purple light ended.

"Your Highness, they are somewhere below us. I will land behind the clump of pine trees, and we can continue our search on the ground," Strongheart stated and proceeded to descend.

Prince Zaaki dismounted Strongheart, placed his sword back in its scabbard and began to walk amongst the picturesque snow-covered pine trees. Strongheart stayed close behind him as they scouted the area for any clues that could lead them to Callum and Panacea. Prince Zaaki stopped near a beautiful hundred-meter-tall pine tree with its needle-like leaves and cones facing upwards and touched its bark. Prince Zaaki closed his eyes and instantly had a vision of Callum, carrying an unconscious Panacea, making his way towards the Stone of Luelza.

Prince Zaaki quickly mounted Strongheart and declared, "Go at once to the Stone of Luelza. They are there."

A confused Strongheart questioned him, "How do you know?"

Prince Zaaki, looking startled, replied, "I had a vision as soon as I touched the pine tree."

"Your Highness, your powers are growing!" Strongheart exclaimed.

"We can discuss this later, but right now, we must go to the Stone of Luelza. There is not a moment to lose," ordered Prince Zaaki as he mounted Strongheart.

Strongheart obeyed and flew like lightening above the pine trees, sensing the urgency in Prince Zaaki's voice. The air became drier and Prince Zaaki and Strongheart found it harder to breath as they neared the Stone of Luelza. It was as if something had sucked all the moisture out of the air.

Strongheart struggled to fly as he fought to take a breath in, hence slowly landed. Luckily, they were a few meters before the Stone of Luelza. Prince Zaaki jumped off Strongheart and ran through the blue snow towards the stone, despite not being able to catch his breath. Strongheart halted for a while to regain his own. As Prince Zaaki ran around the gigantic Stone of Luelza, he found Callum kneeling on the snow with his wife draped over his arms. Prince Zaaki took off his coat and knelt by their side as he covered Panacea with it.

"The Sanquito dragons are after us. They absorb all the moisture from the air. That's why it's so hard for us to breath. I I couldn't walk anymore. And my wife. My wife, she fainted," Callum said breathlessly.

"What is your name?" Prince Zaaki asked, trying to catch his breath.

"I am Callum, and this is Panacea," Callum answered as he began to close his eyes.

Prince Zaaki saw that Callum was about to go unconscious and took Panacea from his arms. Suddenly, Callum collapsed on the blue snow as it began to melt.

Callum, in his tattered clothes and shoes, had long dark brown curly hair and Prince Zaaki clearly saw the resemblance of Ivory and Immanuel.

"Strongheart, come quick," Prince Zaaki beckoned.

Strongheart appeared almost instantaneously.

"Panacea, please wake! You are out of harm's way now, and I will take you to your children. They are all safe and well. Please! Your children are worried about you and miss you tremendously," Prince Zaaki whispered softly into Panacea's ear as he gently lay her on Strongheart's back.

Desperately trying to open her eyes, she nodded in acknowledgement.

"I can see where Ivory gets her beautiful white-blue eyes," Prince Zaaki stated as he saw Panacea's eyes open.

Panacea gradually lifted herself upright on Strongheart's

back.

Prince Zaaki turned to Callum and lifted his head as he tried frantically to wake him. Callum opened his eyes within a few moments and immediately asked for Panacea.

Prince Zaaki reassured Callum as he helped him up and towards Strongheart, "She is awake and on Strongheart. I will take you both to safety now. Your children are all secure and waiting for you. I will deal with the Sanquito dragons later. My priority is to get you to shelter and without delay. We must hurry as the snow is melting, which means the Sanquito dragons are near!"

Callum mounted Strongheart and wrapped his arms around Panacea, to stop her from falling off.

"Strongheart, are you able to fly us to Pos Island?" Prince Zaaki asked, worried for his strength.

"Of course, Your Highness. Jump on! The sooner we leave this area, the better we will all feel," Strongheart declared.

"Open the doors of the Zenith Temple!" Goddess Lulu proclaimed as she floated towards the entrance. Her words magically opened the doors and Strongheart flew in carrying Callum, Panacea and Prince Zaaki on his back.

Goddess Lulu used her powers to move Panacea onto the floating cloud by her side. The Goddess held Panacea's hand and felt the strength of her healing powers. She then proceeded to mystically move Callum onto her floating cloud as well.

"Thank you both for bringing Karena's parents to safety. We will take good care of them," Goddess Lulu praised Strongheart and Prince Zaaki.

"We must return to the Royal Palace at once. My father called for my presence. I must oversee the construction of an energy supply to the Kingdom of Yistyyim," Prince Zaaki informed the Goddess.

"Be safe, my dear Prince and Strongheart," Goddess Lulu bid them farewell and floated through the hallway of the TransM School.
Callum turned to look at Prince Zaaki and called out, "Thank you for saving us. We are forever in your debt!"

Prince Zaaki gave him a nod of acknowledgment as he whispered in Strongheart's ear, "We have no time to lose now. My father will most certainly be losing his patience if we do not return to the palace immediately."

"But Your Highness, what about the Sanquito dragons?" asked Strongheart with a great deal of concern.

"I will send Protectius and some of the army to deal with them as soon as we arrive home," replied Prince Zaaki.

As they were about to leave, Jamilietta appeared in the hallway from behind a large white marble pole. She ran up to Prince Zaaki quietly beckoning him, "Prince Zaaki, please wait!"

Prince Zaaki looked to see who was calling him and replied, "Yes, Jamilietta, is everything well with you and Fred?"

"Yes, Your Highness, Fred and I are both well. Thank you for bringing us here. Fred is learning to use his powers and enjoying his time here. He is so much happier, and I could not thank you enough. Everyone is so welcoming and kind here and I feel very blessed to be in the presence of the Goddesses. Is Protectius well?"

"He is in good health and now the head of the Royal Army at the Royal Palace. I have not told him about Fred. Do you want me to tell him or give him a message or at least inform him that you are alive and safe?" Prince Zaaki questioned her.

Jamilietta looked into Prince Zaaki's captivating eyes and began to weep. She could not hold it in any longer.

Jamillietta began to explain her past actions to Prince Zaaki. "He is my husband, but I left Protectius before he knew I was pregnant. I was worried he might leave me when he discovered that I have a gift. I had a burning feeling that I would pass my gift onto my unborn baby, and I did not want to hurt him or burden him with this."

Prince Zaaki saw the tears rolling down her cheeks and comfortingly said, "I understand your worries and what led you to leaving. You should be telling Protectius all of this."

Jamillietta lowered her head as she wiped the tears from her face.

She looked up at Prince Zaaki and said, "I love him and wish there were a way to tell him, for him to understand that our gifts are not anything bad. I was wrong in disappearing and know I should have stayed and told him, and we could have worked all of this out together. But in a way, I am relieved that we are in this school and amongst others like us. Goddess Ella says that we all have unique gifts that need to be nurtured and treasured and that we must use them wisely, not hide them away. I have come to accept my gift and use it for good. I wish I could share all of the experiences Fred and I have had at the TransM School with Protectius. It is time for him to know the truth."

Prince Zaaki gave Jamilietta a warm embrace and said, "Of course I can tell Protectius that both you and Fred are safe from harm, but I cannot reveal this place to him or anyone. That would put you and everyone here, including the Goddesses, in jeopardy."

"No, it has to come from me. I must tell him, and I will. I will ask Goddess Ella how to visit Protectius with Fred," Jamilietta boldly replied as she wiped away the continuous tears streaming down her cheeks.

"Tell Goddess Ella to inform me of when you would like to visit him. Then I will arrange it for you and Fred to stay at the Royal Palace. Maybe you can even attend the

Battle of the Kingdoms, I am sure that Fred would enjoy that," suggested Prince Zaaki.

"That sounds wonderful. Thank you, Prince Zaaki," Jamilietta whispered and then hurried back down the hallway.

An ambience of elegance and grace filled the evening air as Queen Tee-Tee entered the dining room of the Royal Palace. Queen Tee-Tee wore a long navy-blue gown with green feathers along the front of the waist and a small cluster of diamonds on the left sleeve to match her extravagant heart-shaped diamond necklace that exuded sheer regality.

"My King, have you been waiting long for my presence?" queried Queen Tee-tee as she took her seat opposite him.

"It seems that all of my family is in agreement on keeping me waiting for their presence. Our son is also late. Extremely late," a perturbed King Zok confessed.

"Do not be troubled, my love, I am sure Zaaki will turn up soon," the Queen reassured him comfortingly before distracting him. "Shall we start dinner?"

King Zok nodded in agreement and immediately, dinner was served.

"You look absolutely breathtaking this evening, my darling wife," King Zok declared lovingly before he took his first bite.

"Thank you, my King. I am pleased that I please you," Queen Tee-Tee acknowledged his praise with a hint of sarcasm.

Abruptly, the doors of the dining room flung open, and Prince Zaaki rushed in. He hastily walked towards the king. "Father, I apologise profusely for my tardiness, but it was all for a good reason. I am ready to start work on the energy supply. Where is Prince Yalem?"

"He has retired for the night. I told him that you will meet him at sunrise to start work," said King Zok.

"Very well then. That gives me this night to regain my energy." Prince Zaaki bowed down to his father and walked towards the Queen where he gave her a kiss on her cheek and sat by her side.

"Have you eaten, dear?" Inquired Queen Tee-Tee lovingly.

"I am absolutely famished, Mother."

"Bring Prince Zaaki some dinner please! Now! My son needs to eat!" Queen Tee-Tee decreed to anyone who might hear.

chapter Seven
VII

A golden tunnel of light permeating through Prince Zaaki's large drapes, accompanied by the melody of the majestic singing Catbirds in the gardens of the Royal Palace, awakened Prince Zaaki from his sleep. Hastily, he got ready and made his way on his gold hoverboard to Protectius' office, as he knew Protectius and Prince Yalem would already be waiting for his presence. Prince Zaaki decided to take the long way, through the gardens of the Palace, and soak in some of the sun's rays and smell the sweet aroma of the exotic flowers in full bloom.

Prince Zaaki reached his destination, stepped of his hoverboard and walked into Protectius' office.

"Good morning to you, Your Highness. Shall we begin?" Protectius asked, eager to start.

"Good morning, Protectius. Good morning, Prince Yalem.

On my return to the palace yesterday evening, I asked for you, but Father informed me that you retired to your suite early last night. I hope you slept well," Prince Zaaki stated as he took a seat next to Prince Yalem.

Prince Zaaki hoped his efforts at hospitality could build a solid relationship between the two princes, and in turn, a solid foundation for the future of the two kingdoms. In doing this, he wished to become better acquainted with Prince Yalem in order to form a mutual respect between them and their Kingdoms.

"Yes, I did sleep very well in fact. I thank you for all your hospitality. It has been an honour to be your guest here at the palace," Prince Yalem replied.

Protectius, on the other hand, was only concerned with the safety of the people of his Kingdom and his army so did not participate in small talk.

Protectius, a giant of a man with his muscles protruding through his army uniform, cleared his throat and began to go through the plan to source energy from the Kingdom of Luella to the Kingdom of Yistyyim. "Let us start with the Pink Crystal Rocks in Magnetia. We can build an underground pipeline from the rocks towards the Sea of Chimor, and then the hard bit comes," Protectius stated. "The Sea of Chimor is full of sharkeels, which are deadly, hence we will need the aid of Goldy and the Sizzlites to build the pipeline in the sea. I have spoken to Guardius and Zaeem, and they will oversee the work in Magnetia."

"That is great," Prince Yalem declared. "I have summoned

two hundred men and women of the Royal Army of Yistyyim to help, and they should be arriving shortly. We can then make our way to Magnetia, and my men can set up camp there to help. They will be bringing with them the materials needed to construct the pipeline."

"Protectius, you will take two hundred of our soldiers to go with Prince Yalem and yourself to Magnetia and commence the construction. I will go to Souls Sea to ask Goldy for their assistance and will meet you in Magnetia tomorrow with the Sizzlites, who can start work on the pipeline in the Sea of Chimor towards the Kingdom of Yistyyim," Prince Zaaki instructed.

"Your Highness, I will only need a hundred and fifty of my soldiers, as Zaeem has gathered up a hundred or so men and women to help. I advise you, for the safety of the King and Queen and the Royal Palace, that I leave most of my army here to protect them. Remember that I have already sent five hundred of my soldiers to the Royal Amphitheatre to start work on the security preparations," informed Protectius.

"Very well. If all is in order, I will make my way to Sizzi Village," Prince Zaaki concurred as he stood up and walked towards the door.

Prince Yalem stood up and followed him. He tapped Prince Zaaki on his shoulder and said, "Thank you, Prince Zaaki, for accommodating my Kingdom's needs. Once the work has started on the pipeline, I am hoping that we can travel to the Royal Amphitheatre and see the preparations for the Battle of the Kingdoms."

"Of course. Protectius, please schedule a meeting in three days for us to meet here and travel together to the Royal Amphitheatre. That should give us enough time to get everyone in place for the construction of the pipeline," said Prince Zaaki as he shook hands with Prince Yalem and exited Protectius' office.

"Prince Yalem, do you want to accompany me to organize my army or wait here for your men and women?" Protectius asked.

"I will come with you. My army should be arriving imminently," Prince Yalem replied, and they both departed Protectius' office.

Protectius gathered his army for a meeting in the front garden of the Royal Palace—which spanned fifty acres of purple grass fields—and informed them of their duties. He chose a hundred and fifty people from his army to accompany him to Magnetia and the rest, five hundred or so soldiers, were given orders to protect the Palace.

As Protectius dismissed his army to their duties, he heard a stampede of horses galloping towards the Royal Palace. In the far distance, he saw a beautiful sea of black stallion horses galloping towards him.

"Prince Yalem, your army is arriving. They can eat and rest for an hour and then we will make our way to Magnetia. I will leave you with them to explain the plan of action while I go and inform the King of our plan," Protectius pronounced as he marched towards the entrance of the Royal Palace.

Prince Yalem welcomed his soldiers as they all dismounted their horses. The soldiers of Yistyyim wore dark grey field uniforms with the peace symbol embroidered on the top left shoulder of their coats.

The peace symbol was the symbol of Yistyyim, and it was the center of their white flag. Prince Yalem led his men and women through the Royal Gardens to the soldiers' dining hall, where they could rest, eat and re-energize. The dining hall was large enough to comfortably seat one thousand soldiers with long lines of wooden tables and benches. Prince Yalem informed his soldiers of the plan to build the pipeline from Magnetia through the Sea of Chimor to the Kingdom of Yistyyim.

He then proceeded to sit down at one of the long rectangular dining tables with his soldiers and ask them about their journey.

"Excuse me, Prince Yalem, may I have a word?" A soldier softly tapped him on his soldier.

Prince Yalem stood up and turned around to look at this soldier, who was wearing a long hood that masked their identity. As the soldier removed the hood covering their face, Prince Yalem was happily surprised to see his confidant and wizardess. As a child, Prince Yalem would secretly go to Sekhme's room, in the basement of the palace, and watch her create spells and potions at King

Salam's request.

"I am so glad you came with them, Sekhme," Prince Yalem said as he ushered her out of the dining hall and into the Royal Gardens.

"I knew you would be in need of my assistance. I hear that the Luellans are going to share their energy supply with us. That is great news," Sekhme stated.

Prince Yalem looked around the garden to see if anyone could hear him before he quietly muttered, "Sekhme, I want to win the Battle of the Kingdoms. With the Kingdom of Luella's energy supply and the new land if I win the battle, our Kingdom will become more powerful that the Kingdom of Luella. Remember what we spoke about in Yistyyim? Did you bring it with you?"

"Yes, I have it, but on who do you want to use it?" Sekhme curiously asked.

"Firstly, we will use it on my soldiers, then when the time comes, we will use it on the Luellan soldiers and the spectators at the Battle of the Kingdoms. I will control their minds, and they will do anything I tell them. I will win this battle for us," Prince Yalem proclaimed before continuing. "So tell me, how will you give them the potion?"

"I have put a spell on the potion, transforming it into a gas, so anyone who inhales it will be infected. From the moment they are infected, you will have complete control of their mind and actions. I have connected it to this," Sekhme stated, removing a small mechanism from her pocket and handing it to Prince Yalem.

"This is a CB, or command band, and it will work once I connect it to the energy supply from the Palace. You input your commands and it will communicate them to anyone infected by the potion. You can wear it on your wrist, ask it to show you where your soldiers are at any time, and you can command soldiers, one or all of them, to do whatever it is you need."

Sekhme switched the CB on and programed it to connect to the energy supply within the Royal Palace. Then she programed it to only take orders from Prince Yalem. After which, Sekhme strapped it on Prince Yalem's wrist.

"Let us go back to my soldiers and you can release the gas potion in the dining hall before we leave for Magnetia. I will give you a signal to let you know I am leaving the room. I also want you to stay here when I go to Magnetia and find an opportunity to release the potion on the Luellan army, then await my return," sniggered Prince Yalem with an evil look.

"I will find a way, my Prince. You know I will do anything you ask of me. I am here to serve you, my master. Very soon, you are going to be the most powerful Prince of all the Kingdoms," cackled Sekhme as she placed her hood over her hair, covering her face.

Prince Yalem and Sekhme re-entered the dining hall where Sekhme walked towards the back. Prince Yalem wandered around, greeting more of his soldiers, before giving a look to Sekhme and casually exiting the room. Sekhme took out a small bottle from the inside pocket of her cloak and removed the lid. An odourless, colourless gas was released and filled the air inside the dining hall.

For a moment, all the soldiers froze, then continued as normal, blissfully unaware that they just inhaled this evil potion.

Star was hand-picking some exquisite peach daisies and white daffodils from the garden while the Girtigs were munching on golden berries from large pink trees adjacent to her. All the while, Star's mind was consumed with Prince Zaaki as she arranged the flowers to decorate Queen Tee-Tee's suite.

"A penny for your thoughts," Prince Yalem said as he approached her.

"Oh, Prince Yalem, you startled me," Star said as she stood up to greet him.

"What a lovely arrangement, almost as beautiful as you," Prince Yalem flattered her.

"Thank you," Star acknowledged shyly.

Star brushed a hair from her face as she proceeded to enquire as to her love's location. "Have you seen Prince Zaaki today?"

"Yes, I saw him earlier, but he left to go and see Goldy in Sizzi Village," replied Prince Yalem.

Star's smile seemed to drift away and disappear with the news of Prince Zaaki's departure, yet again.

"Star, I have some work in Magnetia today, but upon my return, I would like to spend more time with you. I see you clearly. Maybe another does not, but I do. You are a rare beauty and should be with someone who can give you the world. I want you on my arm, and if you choose me then I will make you more powerful than you could ever dream. Do not waste your time with Prince Zaaki," Prince Yalem said crassly.

Star was stunned to silence at his words, so much so that the flowers slipped through her fingers and onto the purple grass.

"Think about it. I will come find you when I return."

Prince Yalem took Star's hand, lifted it up towards his lips all the while maintaining eye contact with her, and kissed it.

"I bid you farewell for now, my beautiful lady," Prince Yalem declared and went on his way.

Star watched him walk towards the soldiers' dining hall before returning to handpicking more daffodils.

~~~~

Prince Yalem commanded his CB to tell his soldiers

to be ready to leave the Royal Palace immediately. Instantaneously, he watched as his army, in unison, marched out of the dining hall and towards their horses. They all mounted their horses, galloped to the front of the Royal Palace and awaited further orders.

Protectius sneaked up on Prince Yalem and whispered in his ear, "I am impressed. Very tidy, your soldiers. My men are on their way, and we can leave promptly."

Protectius and Prince Yalem mounted their horses and summoned their armies to follow them. The two rode side by side through the luscious purple fields of the Kingdom of Luella.

Protectius engaged in polite conversation with Prince Yalem, telling him about the history of Magnetia as they rode.

chapter Eight
VIII

Zaeem welcomed Protectius with a manly embrace as he said, "I am glad to see you looking well, Protectius. The head of the Royal Army suits you."

"It is good to be back, my dear friend," replied Protectius.

Zaeem looked at the army behind Protectius and said with a raised voice, "Welcome to Magnetia! We have set up camps for you all to get a good night's rest before starting work in the morning."

"Zaeem, I want you to meet Prince Yalem of Yistyyim. His soldiers will be helping us construct this pipeline," Protectius said as Prince Yalem shook hands with Zaeem.

"It is late, and I am sure you and your men are tired. We will meet at sunrise, after you rest," Zaeem suggested.

Prince Yalem agreed and proceeded to one of the tents to sleep.

Protectius waited for Prince Yalem to enter his tent before asking Zaeem for a private conversation.

"What is it, Protectius? Are the King and Queen safe and well?" Zaeem inquired.

"Yes, yes, they are fine, at least for the time being. I am not quite sure, but I have a feeling Prince Yalem is not here peacefully. I overheard him talking to one of his soldiers, but she did not look like a soldier. I saw her place something on his wrist and heard her say that he could control minds with it. I need you to investigate Prince Yalem, but tell no one, at least until we know for certain if he is here to cause disruption," Protectius shared with concerned caution.

"I will send Guardius to the Kingdom of Yistyyim at once to find out all he can. And in the meantime, I will keep a close eye on the prince myself," Zaeem insisted as he put his arm around Protectius' shoulder.

"Thank you, I can always count on you," Protectius replied.

"Now you must get some rest as well. It will be a long day of work tomorrow," spoke Zaeem as he led Protectius to his tent.

The heat from the blazing red sun was overpowering, so Protectius ordered his army, who were working above ground a few meters from the Pink Crystal Rocks, to take a break from work on the pipeline. The shafts of light beaming from the crystal rocks were magnificent, and Protectius took a moment to appreciate its splendour. He began to recall when he took Jamilietta to this place when they were courting. He remembered how beautiful she looked running around the Pink Crystal Rocks and how much they laughed and talked about the life they would share together. They held hands and watched the sunset; it was his perfect day of happiness and tranquility with the love of his life.

Zaeem and Prince Yalem were with the Yistyyim army in the underground tunnels laying down the pipes leading to the Sea of Chimor. Luckily, there was a cool breeze sweeping through the tunnels that made it bearable for them to work. They were all working together efficiently to build this spectacular pipeline that would lead from one kingdom to the other.

It was halfway through the day and Strongheart, with Prince Zaaki mounted on his back, landed in Magnetia.

Not too far behind was Goldy riding her water leopard, Talgy. They were greeted by Protectius who explained to them the work that had commenced.

"There are over a thousand Sizzlites in the Sea of Chimor awaiting your instructions. They are ready to build the pathway for the pipeline from our kingdom to the Kingdom of Yistyyim," Goldy notified Protectius, with her piercing pink eyes glistening under the rays of the bright sun.

"We appreciate your help, Goldy. Follow me and I will get you some food and water. Prince Zaaki, Zaeem wanted to see you when you arrived. He is in the underground tunnels working alongside Prince Yalem and his army," Protectius said, pointing Prince Zaaki in the direction of the entrance to the tunnels.

"I will make my way there now. Can you please take Strongheart as he needs to drink some water and rest? I also need to have a word with you, Protectius, at some point today," requested Prince Zaaki before he made his way towards the tunnels.

Protectius nodded and led Goldy, Talgy and Strongheart to the camp. Prince Zaaki made his way underground and followed the tunnels until he found some men working on the pipeline and asked them where Zaeem and Prince Yalem were. They pointed him in the right direction and Prince Zaaki continued down one of the tunnels.

Finally, Prince Zaaki reached Zaeem and immediately Zaeem, happy to see him, gave him a warm Magnetian embrace.

"You look well, Prince Zaaki. We have missed you in Magnetia. I wanted to discuss a personal matter with you regarding Fred, that little boy who used to visit my son," said Zaeem under his breath so no one could hear him.

"Tell me, what is this matter? But first, tell me how Prince Yalem and his army are getting on?" Prince Zaaki asked curiously.

"Prince Yalem is working hard alongside my men and his. We are right on schedule, although it is very early days. This pipeline should be complete in Magnetia in a week or so, permitting no problems arise." Zaeem pondered on their task for a moment before going on to query, "I was talking with Bobby, and he told me that Fred's father is Protectius. Is that true?"

"I am not at liberty to answer that."

"Then, at least tell me if Jamilietta is well and safe. Protectius still loves her very much, and I know that she will always be in his heart. I worry for him. I know he misses her, and he should know he has a son," Zaeem said passionately.

"Zaeem, Jamilietta and Fred are in a safe place. That much I can tell you. Jamilietta will tell Protectius in her own time. Do not worry; the time will be sooner than you think," Prince Zaaki reassured Zaeem.

"Very well."

"I am in need of your assistance. There are Sanquito Dragons in the Great Snow Blue Mountain, and I want you to accompany Protectius and myself tomorrow to find them. They were involved in the kidnapping of Callum and Panacea, who I have safely rescued, but I was not able to stay behind and stop these dragons from kidnapping others or causing more disturbance."

Zaeem looked shocked as the return of dragons worried him greatly. "I am deeply saddened to hear that there are more dragons lurking in our Kingdom. Can the Luellan army help?"

"I wanted to send some of my army to find and capture these dragons, but I fear these dragons are not easily defeated. Therefore, I want us to go investigate and find out as much as we can about them. Will you be able to leave here for a day or two?" requested Prince Zaaki.

"Without hesitation, Your Highness. Do you know anything about these dragons?" asked Zaeem, very intrigued.

"Yes, I have some information on them, and I will tell you all I know on our journey," Prince Zaaki said as he shook Zaeem's hand and walked away.

At the break of dawn, Protectius and Zaeem mounted their horses and followed Strongheart and Prince Zaaki as they made their way towards the Great Snow Blue Mountain. The horses galloped in sync, side by side, tearing through the picturesque purple fields at high speed. During their journey, Prince Zaaki relayed all his knowledge on the Sanquito Dragons to Protectius and Zaeem. Without any breaks, they arrived at the black pyramid-like Royal Stone of Luelza just before sunset.

"The air is dry again, which means the Sanquito Dragons are close. I do not know how many there are, but I know that they travel in large groups. We must find out who has conjured them and why they kidnapped Panacea and Callum. Remember what I told you: they are bat-like dragons which bite and spit with the deadliest of venom. Their venom will kill you instantly, so beware and keep your distance at all times," Prince Zaaki whispered to Protectius and Zaeem.

"Zaeem, I will need you to hide behind the stone, and only on my signal come out. Protectius, you and I will attempt to talk to them first, and if they attack, then be ready to fight back," continued Prince Zaaki.

"I sense them near, Your Highness. They are approaching us and there are five that I can see," Strongheart stated as he looked up and saw them in the distance.

The Sanquito Dragons had charcoal lizard-like skin and flew like bats. When their wings flapped together, it created a continuous disturbing high-pitched noise.

"Get ready, Strongheart. I know it is hard to breathe as they approach us, but try to stay strong and persist," said Prince Zaaki, struggling to take in a deep breath as he removed his sword from its scabbard.

Prince Zaaki raised the hood of his cloak over his head as the Sanquito Dragons landed in front of him. Protectius and Prince Zaaki, both mounted on their horses, lowered their swords.

"Why are you here?" Prince Zaaki demanded.

"We are here for you, Prince Zaaki," one of the Sanquito dragons replied.

"You want me? Who sent you?" Prince Zaaki asked curiously.

The Sanquito dragons sniggered and said together, "The General, of course."

"The General? General Scarytis you mean? He is dead! I am losing patience now. What did you want with Callum and Panacea?" Prince Zaaki shouted.

"We have no use for them now. Panacea did what we needed, and Callum told us what he saw. If we require Panacea's services again, we will find her."

Prince Zaaki realized in that moment why they were kidnapped, and under his breath, he said, "You used them. Panacea to heal the General " Prince Zaaki paused for a moment before continuing. "And Callum, you used him to foresee the future. I demand you take us to the General at once."

"We cannot do that. We are under orders to let you go, but we have a message from the General. Beware of the Battle of the Kingdoms: he will be waiting at every corner for you. None of you are safe. He will get his revenge," one of the Sanquito Dragons replied, and subsequently, they all flew away.

"Shall we follow them?" Protectius asked Prince Zaaki.

"No, let them go. But we must be prepared for an attack during the battle. Protectius, you will ride back with Zaeem to Magnetia, get Prince Yalem and then meet me tomorrow at the Royal Amphitheatre. Zaeem, will you be able to take the lead in the pipeline construction with Goldy?" asked a very concerned Prince Zaaki.

"Most certainly, Your Highness. Where are you going?" Zaeem replied.

"I must go see someone to find out more about the General and if it is possible that he survived," Prince Zaaki answered as he tapped Strongheart on his back. Without delay, Strongheart swiftly flew towards their destination.

"Why are you here, Prince Zaaki?" Goddess Lulu asked.

"I need to ask you an important question. Is it possible that General Scarytis is still alive? When he attempted to take over the Kingdom of Luella, capturing my parents and holding them prisoners in the Royal Palace, I fought him and stabbed him with my sword, piercing his heart.

He stopped breathing. Not just that, we buried him. How can it be?" Prince Zaaki questioned, thoroughly bewildered and losing his composure.

"Take a deep breath and calm down, my dear Prince Zaaki. You must try to not let yourself become agitated. You are beginning to see the challenges and battles we face quite regularly." Goddess Lulu took a short pause to allow Prince Zaaki to settle down before continuing, "Let me see what I can find out."

Goddess Lulu closed her eyes and focused on the time of General Scarytis' death, whilst Prince Zaaki intently watched her.

A vision came to Goddess Lulu, and she allowed it to play out before replying, "He was protected by a witch who had put a spell on him. In the event of injury or death, she had a window of time to find his body, reverse the severe injury and heal him. She found where he was buried and performed a spell on his corpse that brought him back to life. These types of witches are difficult for us to locate and trace. They put invisible barriers around themselves to prevent us from recognizing or finding them. I will keep trying to see the witch's face, but at the moment, it is blurred. It seems like she is with him now, so it is impossible for me locate General Scarytis' current location."

Goddess Lulu closed her eyes and raised her hands to face-level, palms facing upwards. A mystical silver fog appeared in her palms, and she softly blew it. The silver fog drifted a few centimeters in front of her. Goddess Lulu opened her eyes and within the fog saw a vision of

General Scarytis, revealing both past and future actions.

"He has conjured over a hundred Sanquito Dragons to protect and serve him. Panacea saved his life. The Sanquito Dragons for this reason kidnapped her. He is preparing to let the Sanquito Dragons attack you and your father, King Zok, at the Battle of the Kingdoms and cause havoc with the competitors. He wants to kill you, Prince Zaaki, and avenge the death of his daughter, Sahara," Goddess Lulu informed Prince Zaaki and Strongheart.

Prince Zaaki's head tilted down to the ground, overcome with sadness and a feeling of great remorse.

The Prince then lifted his head and explained, "Sahara was working with her evil father to kill my parents and take Star hostage. There was no other way. I feel the pain of her death every day, especially because she is Star's sister. But in saving Star from Sahara's capture, I fought and killed Sahara."

Goddess Lulu responded to his actions, "We all have decisions to make in life. Sometimes one can think them through wisely, and sometimes one must act on instinct. You saved the life of the woman you love, and the consequence of that was the death of Sahara. You must find it within yourself to accept this and move on."

"I know you are right, but it is hard to see Star and not remember fighting her twin sister," Prince Zaaki sighed.

Goddess Lulu comfortingly said, "We are in a time of imminent danger and evil taking over. You did what you had to do to protect the good people of the Kingdom of Luella. I do not want to see you torture yourself with this."

Prince Zaaki graciously replied, "Thank you for your words of wisdom as always, Goddess Lulu."

"Now let me get back to the vision before me. I see him searching for Star during the battle. I see him standing behind your father. You need to ensure the safety of the King, the Queen and Star during the battle. Goddess Ella and I will be bringing some of our extremely gifted children with us to watch the battle incognito, so we will be able to help should the General and the Sanquito Dragons appear and attack," said Goddess Lulu to try and reassure Prince Zaaki.

"I do not want to put you in harm's way. I can fight this battle alone. Please stay here with the children and stay out of danger. I will deal with this," insisted Prince Zaaki.

"Prince Zaaki, you forget that Goddess Ella and I are Goddesses, therefore immortal and nothing can harm us. We will be there for you. No need to worry for our safety, I have that under control. Now be on your way. I will send you and Strongheart back to the Royal Palace," Goddess Lulu said and held out her right hand for Prince Zaaki to grasp.

"Strongheart, come to my left side please," Goddess Lulu ordered kindly.

Goddess Lulu touched Strongheart's back with her left

hand and recited a spell in Libnene, "Nielon hala ala beitoun, Nielon hala ala beitoun."

Suddenly, Prince Zaaki and Strongheart vanished.

A new dawn was breaking, and Prince Zaaki awoke to find himself in his bed. He rushed to get ready and go to the royal stables to find Strongheart.

"Strongheart, did you rest well?" Prince Zaaki asked as he began to brush Strongheart's beautiful purple coat and his silver mane.

"Yes, Your Highness. We have much to do today. Are we going to the Royal Amphitheatre?" Strongheart inquired.

"Yes, after we eat. I must go see my parents at breakfast and then we will head out," Prince Zaaki said as he continued to brush Strongheart's mane.

"Prince Zaaki, I will not let anything happen to you, and I will fight with you to protect the King and Queen. I will never leave your side," Strongheart stated boldly.

"Strongheart, I do not worry for myself. I worry for those I love and care about. But I have a plan, and I will go see Futuris on our return from the Royal Amphitheatre."

"Prince Zaaki!" Star called out as she walked through the hallway and towards the breakfast room of the Royal Palace.

Prince Zaaki turned around and saw Star. He ran to her, lifting her up off the ground and twirling her around, before placing her gently back on the ground.

"I have missed you, my love. How have you been?" Prince Zaaki asked her as he gazed into her eyes.

"I have missed you tremendously. What has been keeping you so busy and far from the palace and from me?" she questioned with a loving look.

"The pipeline from Magnetia to the Kingdom of Yistyyim. And today, I am to go to the Royal Amphitheatre to check on the preparations for the Battle of the Kingdoms," Prince Zaaki responded as he lifted both her hands up to his lips and softly placed a kiss on each hand.

Star wrapped her arms around Prince Zaaki's neck and gave him a loving embrace.

"I wake up every morning thinking of you, wishing and hoping that you are here in the palace so I can see you," Star said caringly.

"Star, you are always on my mind and in my heart.

Although I may not be around as much due to my obligations and responsibilities, my love for you grows with every day. Please know that once the Battle of the Kingdoms is over, I pledge my time to you. But for now, I must go and find my parents. Have you seen them?"

"I just left Queen Tee-Tee in her suite. She will be coming to breakfast shortly, and King Zok should already be at breakfast," Star replied.

"I must go talk to my father now. On my return this evening from the Amphitheatre, may I escort you for a stroll around the gardens?" Prince Zaaki asked.

Star nodded as she looked up into his eyes and longed for him to kiss her, and without a second's thought of his lips upon hers, he kissed her farewell.

Prince Zaaki proceeded to walk into the breakfast dining room to find King Zok reading some documents whilst munching on some exotic fruits.

"Father, good morning," Prince Zaaki said as he bowed and took a seat next to his father. "Anything worthy that you are so consumed with this morning?"

"My son, I am just going over some of the paperwork the judges sent me regarding the Battle of the Kingdoms. It seems as though there will be new games involved," replied King Zok.

"The pipeline construction is going smoothly, and the Sizzlites are helping create a pathway in the Sea of Chimor. I have left Zaeem in charge and Protectius will accompany Prince Yalem to meet me at the Amphitheatre this morning," Prince Zaaki informed his father.

"Great work you are doing, my son. I am very proud of you, indeed. I am not sure if I have told you the story of the Royal Amphitheatre before. I designed it before you were born, and construction began while your mother was pregnant with you. It was completed on your first birthday. We invited guests to attend your first birthday in the Royal Amphitheatre. It was a wonderful day. Anyway, enough of reliving history, let us eat. Your mother should be joining us shortly," King Zok stated as he reached into his fruit bowl.

"Father, I will be organizing more security around you and mother during the battle. Nothing to be concerned about, but I feel it is necessary," Prince Zaaki casually stated.

"Very well," King Zok acknowledged his son's instructions and continued with his breakfast.

"Good morning, my two favourite men. It is a wonderful morning to be greeted by my husband and my son," Queen Tee-Tee declared as she gracefully entered the dining room.

"Good morning, Mother," Prince Zaaki replied as he stood up to walk over to his mother and plant a kiss on her cheek. "I do not have long before I must make my way to the Royal Amphitheatre."

"Any time I spend with you is indeed an honour, my dear boy. I am happy to see you working hard so the

Battle of the Kingdoms will be a great success for our Kingdom," said Queen Tee-Tee.

Strongheart flew Prince Zaaki, above purple fields filled with orange and red wild trees, eighty miles south of the Royal Palace to the Royal Amphitheatre. Strongheart landed in the middle of the stage, and Prince Zaaki dismounted his horse, gazing around at the spectacular sight of this colossal stadium. The Royal Amphitheatre had tiered, white stone seating for over two thousand spectators that encircled the stage, where the battle was to take place. The spectacular open-air oval glistened majestically under the bright rays of the red sun. Today the magical stage was being transformed into four transparent rooms for four rounds of battles. Prince Zaaki heard Protectius commanding some of the Luellan army under the spectators' seats, hence he walked over to the tunnel leading to the preparation rooms under the Amphitheatre.

"You are here, at last. I want to introduce you to the five judges that have travelled from other kingdoms to be here for the Battle of the Kingdoms," Protectius said loudly as he began to introduce Prince Zaaki and Prince Yalem to the impartial judges.

Prince Yalem and Prince Zaaki shook all their hands as Protectius introduced them one by one, "This is Aadeh, the judge from here in the Kingdom of Luella. He was a well-respected advisor for King Zok, and now that he is retired, he has happily agreed to be the head judge on this occasion. This is Jugor from the Kingdom of Yistyyim. This is Domero from the Kingdom of Sorreno. This is Taress from the Kingdom of Tranquily and this is Kastis from the Kingdom of Roderna."

"It is an honour to meet you all. I am grateful that you have all travelled a long way to be here," Prince Yalem exclaimed.

"Here, here. I agree with my friend, Prince Yalem. Now, shall we go to the judges' conference room and discuss the plan of events for the big day?" Prince Zaaki asked, eager to find out as much as possible about the details of this event.

Protectius agreed and led them all into a room where they sat down and went through the events of the day. Prince Zaaki insisted that every minute of the day was thoroughly organised, hence Prince Zaaki knew where every soldier and competitor was. After many hours of planning, the judges briefly ended the meeting with a brief description of the winning prize, which was the co-ordinates to the new-found island to be revealed at the end of the battle.

After a long and tiring day of planning, Prince Zaaki, Prince Yalem and Protectius returned to the Royal Palace for dinner with the King and Queen of Luella.

Prince Zaaki, exhausted, retired to his suite to rest. Out of nowhere, his balcony doors swung open, and Goddess Lulu floated in on her luscious white cloud.

"I am here to inform you of the importance of the Battle of the Kingdoms. The new-found land is to the southeast of Pos Island and very close to us. It is imperative that you win this battle and keep anyone from travelling to this new island. It is overgrown with forests of the most magnificent cedar trees that are under our protection, but I am afraid that whoever wins will turn the island into homes for people and a venture sight. This will put our sacred TransM School at risk of being discovered. We need your help so that Goddess Ella and myself do not have to intervene. I have faith that you will win this battle, but now more than ever this battle is worth not just a new island but also our holy land, the City of SADK," Goddess Lulu conveyed emotionally.

Prince Zaaki, overwhelmed at the amount of pressure placed on his shoulders, sat down on the side of his bed to take it all in.

"Prince Zaaki, you are not alone in this. We will be by your side and help you when you need us. Do not forget that. Call for us and we will hear you. I am aware that you have an engagement now with Star and so I will leave, but I will be summoning you during the night to show you a TransM ceremony taking place. It is time for you to start your journey of knowledge of souls." Goddess Lulu voiced as she floated out of his balcony doors and disappeared.

Prince Zaaki sat on the edge of his bed for a few moments to absorb this new information regarding the new-found island. After which, he washed and changed his clothes and made his way on his hoverboard to the gardens where Star was anxiously awaiting his presence.

Prince Yalem secretly watched the Royal family retire to their suites before creeping out of the Royal Palace, through the gardens of the palace and into the soldiers' quarters where Sekhme was staying. He found Sekhme sound asleep and nudged her awake. Sekhme slowly opened her eyes and saw Prince Yalem standing in front of her.

"What is the matter, Your Highness?" Sekhme whispered.

"Did you do what I asked?" Prince Yalem murmured.

"Yes! I successfully infected the majority of them when they were having their dinner. I then waited until the remaining few, who were on late duty, retired for the night and I contaminated them when they fell asleep," Sekhme bragged.

"Now that I have control of the Luellan and Yistyyim

Army, my plan to win the battle is coming together. Go back to sleep and I will find you tomorrow," Prince Yalem quietly ordered as he departed the soldiers' quarters.

chapter Nine
IX

Prince Zaaki was sleeping peacefully in his bed when an over-powering electric silver beam encompassed his whole body, abruptly awakening him. He tried to fight it and escape, but then he heard Goddess Lulu's voice in his mind telling him to stay calm. Prince Zaaki refrained from attempting to escape this beam and closed his eyes. He composed himself and allowed it to magically transport him to a TransM room on Pos Island. He found himself standing adjacent to Goddess Ella and Goddess Lulu.

"Welcome, Prince Zaaki," Goddess Ella warmly greeted him. "We transported you here, into the sacred TransM room. Goddess Lulu informed me that you are ready to see exactly what it is that we do here. There are three parts to the soul: the reason, the spirit and the desire. The TransM angels assess each soul and then place it in a new body, about to be born. It is not only the decision of the TransM angels, for primarily, it is the soul's decision. The soul has made choices and decisions in its previous life that determine the new life it is born into. There are many levels, and it is through knowledge, wisdom, valuing the importance of life, kindness, love, compassion, learning and teaching, that each soul climbs up the levels to reach the ultimate knowledge of life and the afterlife," Goddess Ella thoroughly explained. She then lifted her hands, palms facing each other, and a silver ball appeared in between her palms.

Goddess Ella gently released the ball onto Karena and Charon who were in mid-air with their golden wings spread. Charon took the silver ball with his hands and spread his palms apart, and a soul appeared, a light grey form of a human body floating.

As the Goddess spoke, her voice echoed in this room with no ceiling. An extraordinary supernatural feeling overwhelmed Prince Zaaki as he stood within its walls.

Goddess Ella resumed to speak, "You will watch Charon, who is only fifteen years of age and from the Kingdom of Sorreno, and Karena, whom you have already met, navigate and guide a travelling soul into a new body. Charon is an Upper TransM angel who has been with us since he was four years old, and Karena is fourteen years of age and is a Lower TransM angel."

Karena took the soul's left hand and Charon took its right hand as they flew higher and higher in this room with no ceiling in sight. They began to swirl around at a speed faster than the eye could see.

Goddess Ella continued to explain the process to Prince

Zaaki, "Now Karena is discussing why the soul made certain decisions in its previous life and the outcomes. If they were good or bad decisions, this does not necessarily dictate their future path. It is more important to see how the soul took responsibility for its actions, rectified them, learned from them, made their lives better and so on. Karena will channel the use of her powers of being able to see into the soul's past and discuss every action and cause and effect the soul had on itself and others. After this is done, the soul will be given a chance to fairly decide its future and where its path will lead it, hence which kind of life it will be born into. Once the decision is decided amongst the soul, Karena and Charon, Charon will guide the soul into a new body. Finally, Karena and Charon will return."

Prince Zaaki stood in awe of this amazing and breathtakingly wondrous sight, completely and utterly speechless. He felt absolutely blessed and honoured to be allowed to watch this extremely emotional journey of this soul.

After it was complete, Karena and Charon flew down and landed in front of the Goddesses and Prince Zaaki.

Goddess Ella addressed Karena and Charon, "That was beautiful! And I am proud of you both. You have both come a long way."

Karena replied, "Thank you, Goddess Ella. I know I am not allowed to speak of what I learned about that soul, but that soul had an overwhelmingly emotional life. It definitely resonated with me."

Karena began to shed a tear but quickly wiped it away.

"I know, Karena, but you learn to not let your own personal emotions get in the way of each soul. Every soul has led a different and unique life, and you will learn to appreciate every life and harness the goodness in each one. You can find goodness in every life, even when you feel that the life is full of bad choices and actions. It was an emotional journey; I do agree with you. Remember we will be together in this. I am there with you and for you as well as being there for the soul," Charon declared inspiringly.

"I am speechless. That was miraculous. And I am in awe of you both," Prince Zaaki declared, still stunned at what had just occurred before his eyes.

"You may go now. Thank you, Karena and Charon," Goddess Lulu dismissed Karena and Charon, and they closed their wings and departed the room.

Goddess Lulu turned to Prince Zaaki and said, "For an ideal Kingdom, in fact an ideal world, every individual will possess the wisdom, justice, courage and self-discipline to live a well-balanced life. To work towards a harmonious world, the leaders, Kings and Queens of a Kingdom, will need to possess and display these qualities and be role models for their people. This will inspire the people to be like them and possess these qualities as well. In a way, the leaders of the kingdoms will be philosophers as well. We are working with other princes and princesses in other kingdoms as well and hope that peace and harmony will prevail throughout the Realm. You have a fight in the near future, and simply, it will be a fight against the bad of the realm. With your powers and knowledge, you will succeed in this fight. No matter how hard it gets, never give up! When you feel like there is no hope left, that is when your faith in the good must be at its highest. Always remember when you need help, do not be afraid to ask for it. We will always be there to help you. You have the support of us and the students in the TransM School."

"Thank you, Goddess Lulu and Goddess Ella. I will need your help during the Battle of the Kingdoms. I am worried about an attack from General Scarytis and his swarms of Sanquito Dragons. I fear for my parents and Star and all the spectators," Prince Zaaki confessed with an apprehensive look on his face.

Prince Zaaki felt a profuse amount of responsibility for the safety of his entire Kingdom and for the visitors coming to watch the Battle of the Kingdoms. He was overwrought with fear of losing someone close to him, but he tried to collect his thoughts and stay composed.

"We are attending the battle and bringing some of our students with us. We will be ready for any attack," Goddess Lulu assured him and continued. "Now we must send you back to the palace. Speak of what you have seen here to no one. One final thing, Prince Zaaki, please know that you are a force to be reckoned with and more powerful than you realise. You have powers within you that will come through when you need them. You can do anything you set your mind to, and you will achieve success in keeping the peace in the Kingdom of Luella and ridding it of evil. Believe in yourself, because Goddess Ella and I believe in you."

Goddess Ella and Goddess Lulu placed the palm of their hands together and a white glow emerged. This blinding white glow began to encompass Prince Zaaki and he was instantaneously transported back into his bed in the Royal Palace.

Futuris opened the doors to Prince Zaaki's suite with a wave of his right hand that caused a forceful breeze. He entered and the doors magically slammed shut behind him.

"Your Highness, please awake. The battle commences the day after tomorrow and you are not ready. I must prepare you!" Futuris demanded as he removed the blanket off Prince Zaaki.

Prince Zaaki, flooded with exhaustion from the stress and worry of the surmountable danger lurking in the very near future, kept his eyes closed and muttered, "Futuris, it is too early for this now. Please let me rest. I will come find you at midday."

"Very well. Very well. I will leave this book of spells with you to glance over before you come find me. You will need these once the battle commences," Futuris reluctantly agreed and left Prince Zaaki's suite.

Prince Zaaki entered Futuris' room in the basement of the palace to find Futuris talking with Progra, the palace's technician. Progra wore big thick spectacles that were almost entirely covered with his long, curly, electric red hair. Futuris, aware of Prince Zaaki's presence, continued to instruct Progra to create impenetrable suits of armour for the King and Queen of Luella.

"Progra, please also make one for Protectius and one for Star," Prince Zaaki asked.

"I will get right on that," Progra replied, and bowing down to Prince Zaaki, he left the room.

"Come here, dear boy," beckoned Futuris to Prince Zaaki.

Prince Zaaki walked over to Futuris who was standing by his large crystal ball. The room was toasty and warm due to the fire crackling in the red brick fireplace.

"Look and tell me what you see," Futuris demanded.

Prince Zaaki stared into the crystal ball and replied, "I see a grey fog."

"Look harder!" insisted Futuris.

"Very well." Prince Zaaki focused on the crystal ball, and images began to emerge. "I see General Scarytis.

And and Father is sitting in the Royal Balcony of the Amphitheatre with Mother by his side. General Scarytis is behind Father and about to stab him with his sword!"

"Yes! That is why I am doing everything I can to prevent this event from happening. You must not leave the battle once it commences, or you forfeit the Kingdom of Luella's place. I have spoken to Protectius, and he is aware of this. He will be King Zok's personal guard on the day of the Battle of the Kingdoms. I am showing you this so you do not jeopardize your place in this important battle. We have it under control. We want your focus to be on winning the battle. Progra is devising an invisible protection blanket to encapsulate King Zok and Queen Tee-Tee and whoever will be with them on the Royal Balcony. We are just not sure if the General can break this shield," Futuris stated.

"I cannot take part in these games if my father's life is at risk. I will not take part in them!" Prince Zaaki demanded furiously.

"This is what the General wants; for the Kingdom to look weak so he can come forth and claim he is the rightful person to become the next King of Luella. I will not allow you to forfeit the Battle of the Kingdoms," Futuris declared.

Prince Zaaki remained silent as he tried to think of ways to protect his father.

Futuris continued to speak, "Also, did you take a look at the book of spells I left with you this morning?"

Prince Zaaki motioned his head to acknowledge he read the spells.

"Any problems with the spells?" Futuris queried.

"No. The spells are fine. Futuris, is there any way you can find out where General Scarytis is hiding? I know it will be near the Great Snow Blue Mountain," Prince Zaaki requested.

"I have already attempted many times to locate his position, but it seems he has a conjurer there protecting him," Futuris uttered in dismay.

"I will go look for him myself now! There is no time to waste!" Prince Zaaki exclaimed as he hurried out of Futuris' room.

"Prince Zaaki! The games are but a day away," Futuris said under his breath, realizing that nothing could stop Prince Zaaki from finding the General and killing him once and for all.

"Star! Star, wait up, I want to talk with you," Prince Yalem called out as he ran to catch up to Star on the stairs leading down to the gardens of the palace.

Star turned around, hoping that it was Prince Zaaki calling her name, but when she saw it was Prince Yalem, her smile turned into a frown. Prince Yalem, catching up with Star, began to ask her about her day and if he could walk with her. She nodded graciously and they continued down the steep staircase into the gardens of the palace.

"Tell me about yourself, Star. You have caught my eye, and that is a rarity. I want to win the battle tomorrow in your honour," Prince Yalem said brashly.

"There is no need for that. As for me, there isn't much to tell. I am the Queen's lady-in-waiting," Star murmured, blushing as she began to pick some flowers from the garden for the Queen's suite.

"Oh, come now, I am sure there is more to you than that. Tell me about your parents. Do you have any siblings?" Prince Yalem inquired.

"I had a twin sister, but she was killed," Star hesitated, realizing what she had said, and she quickly stopped herself from saying any more.

"I am sorry to hear that. If you don't mind me asking, how was she killed?" Prince Yalem couldn't help himself from asking this insensitive question.

"She was not a good person. I suppose she took after my father, General Scarytis, who used to be King Zok's General, right here at the palace. When he tried to overthrow the King and take his place, Prince Zaaki stopped him. Unfortunately, both my father and sister were killed. I know what they did was wrong and hurt many people, but I still did not wish them dead," Star shed a few tears as she spoke, and Prince Yalem comforted her in his arms.

"I was not aware of this. My deepest condolences. I am sure this must put a strain on your relationship with Prince Zaaki. Does he know of your feelings?" Prince Yalem whispered in her ear as he continued to embrace her.

Star pulled away from his arms and replied, "Prince Zaaki and I are just perfect! And there is nothing for him to know. We are perfect. Just perfect!" Star insisted and continued picking flowers and arranging them.

"Oh, that is good then. I am sorry if I said anything to offend you. Thank you for the walk, and I will leave you in peace. Good day, my beautiful lady," Prince Yalem said as he walked away.

Prince Yalem rushed to the soldiers' quarters to find Sekhme sitting on a stool with her eyes closed.

"Sekhme, I need you to find the location of the body of General Scarytis," Prince Yalem demanded. "Right now, Sekhme!"

Sekhme continued to keep her eyes closed and responded, "Wait for a moment, please. I am conjuring a spell."

A moment passed and she opened her eyes and took out a map of Luella from her pocket and placed in upon her lap. She removed the locket from around her neck and held it above the map.

"Find the body of General Scarytis," she repeated five times, faintly.

The locket moved around the map and landed in a place called Ardmiya.

"He is not dead," Sekhme stated as she strongly felt his presence.

"What do you mean he is not dead?" inquired Prince Yalem.

"He is most certainly alive and breathing."

"That is great, actually. We must meet with him at once. Can you take me to this place, Ardmiya?" Prince Yalem asked impatiently.
Sekhme nodded.

"There is no time to waste, Sekhme! Let us leave now!" insisted Prince Yalem.

chapter Ten
X

It was the day before the Battle of the Kingdoms and Prince Zaaki felt defeated that his search yesterday for General Scarytis came to no avail. He lay on his couch with his balcony doors wide open to let in a soft breeze. He sulked, not knowing what to do. He thought to himself that he could not stop his father from attending this momentous occasion that happened once every few years. Especially since the battle was being held in his own Kingdom for the very first time.

Abruptly, Protectius barged into Prince Zaaki's suite with Guardius following closely behind him.

"Your Highness, Guardius has just returned from the Kingdom of Yistyyim and has some valuable information about Prince Yalem," Protectius proclaimed.

"Who sent you, Guardius, to Yistyyim?" Prince Zaaki asked.

"Your Highness." Guardius bowed to the prince, and then continued, "Zaeem instructed me to go."

Protectius interrupted him. "I sent him. I had my suspicions about Prince Yalem and informed Zaeem. Zaeem and I decided to send Guardius to find out what he could."

"Tell me then what you discovered," Prince Zaaki demanded.

"Prince Yalem was found at the doorstep of the Royal Palace of Yistyyim one late night by the Queen's lady-in-waiting. The King and Queen searched for his parents unsuccessfully, so they raised him as their own. I spoke with some of the servants in the palace, and they informed me that Prince Yalem was a difficult child. He was stubborn and always setting things on fire. He burned down their stables, and four of the royal horses were killed. The King and Queen of Yistyyim patiently tried to teach him and guide him, even hiring a wizardess to help him control his anger and rage. Her name is Sekhme, and she is here in our Kingdom with the Yistyyim soldiers. One of the servants informed me that Sekhme is not a good wizardess, as originally thought, as she is in possession of evil spells and potions. I am afraid that she informed me that she overheard Prince Yalem and Sekhme plotting to win the Battle of the Kingdoms and take over the Kingdom of Luella. She was unable to hear the whole conversation, but she heard something about controlling both of our armies' minds. Protectius had heard this same thing," Guardius informed Prince Zaaki.

Prince Zaaki, angered by this new knowledge, stood up from his couch and grabbed his sword, which was leaning against the wall in its scabbard. He then walked towards the door and turned around to Protectius and Guardius.

"Where are you going?" probed Protectius. "If you are going to seek out Prince Yalem and interrogate him, I advise against it!"

"Why?" Prince Zaaki bellowed.

"I have a plan, Your Highness." Protectius stood up, walked over to Prince Zaaki and put his arm comfortingly around his shoulder. "A plan to rid us of General Scarytis and the Sanquito Dragons and to capture Prince Yalem in his evil plot. King Zok and Queen Tee-Tee will be safe and unharmed, I swear this on my life."

"Well then, take a seat and tell me," Prince Zaaki ordered as he led them to his living room where they all rested on armchairs.

Protectius began to elaborate in detail on his plan and produced a detailed map of the Royal Amphitheatre, which he hung on the wall in front of them. Guardius, Prince Zaaki and Protectius worked on the plan for hours, with Prince Zaaki calling for Progra to join them. Progra brought with him some devices he had created, thinking they could be helpful.

Whilst Protectius was talking, Prince Zaaki suddenly had a vision of Goddess Ella telling him of their meeting and who from the TransM School would be in attendance at the battle. The vision only lasted for a few moments, after which Prince Zaaki disclosed this vision to Protectius, Guardius and Progra, explaining to them only what they needed to know without disclosing any information regarding the TransM School.

They all worked late into the night, preparing for the looming attack and various plans of defense for different scenarios.

Meanwhile at the TransM School, Goddess Ella and Goddess Lulu called for a meeting with Panacea, Jamilietta, Fred, Baal, Karena and Immanuel, who had recently began to discover powers of his own, to prepare them for the Battle of the Kingdoms. The Goddesses explained of a highly possible attack from the Sanquito Dragons and General Scarytis against the Royal Family and the spectators at the battle.

All the while, Goddess Ella telepathically communicated what was discussed at this meeting with Prince Zaaki.

Star knocked on Queen Tee-Tee's door and waited for the guards to open it before she entered. Star curtsied to the Queen.

"Star, I thought we might talk over tea on my balcony, seeing as it is such a lovely day," Queen Tee-Tee suggested as she wandered over to her balcony.

Star followed her and replied, "Certainly, Your Majesty."

The Queen's elegance and poise slightly intimidated Star as she sat opposite the Queen. Star poured out some tea into the Queen's cup first and added a small spoon of honey. As she poured herself a cup, the Queen began to question her about her feelings towards Prince Zaaki.

"Prince Zaaki is wonderful, Your Majesty. He is so caring and attentive when we are together, but of late I have hardly seen him. He is extremely preoccupied with the Battle of the Kingdoms and constructing the pipeline and he has little time to spend with me," Star expressed.

Queen Tee-Tee replied, "My dear, he is heir to the throne and must learn what is involved with running a Kingdom. His time will be primarily for the good people of our Kingdom. I have stood by King Zok's side since we were married, and I am well aware of the responsibilities and duties of a king. I waited patiently for time alone with my husband, but when he was preoccupied with kingdom affairs, I delved into work of my own."

Star was intrigued and asked, "What did you do to make the time pass until you were with him again?" Star took a short pause before resuming, " if you do not mind me asking, Your Majesty."

Queen Tee-Tee smiled and said, "Of course not. I planted fruits and vegetables in the garden, and when they were in full season, I began to send them to villages around the Kingdom. I also set up meetings with village leaders to discuss ways to help each other. I organised the best events for people of the kingdom to mingle and, most importantly, to stay united."

Queen Tee-Tee took a sip from her tea. Star followed suit, gulping down her tea, quickly finishing it.

Queen Tee-Tee placed her cup down and said, "What I am telling you, my dear, is that his love for you is as strong as ever and will not fade. However, the love for his kingdom and his duty as heir to the throne will take him away from you for periods of time. Know that he will always return and need your love and support through it all. There are many things you can occupy yourself with here. What interests you?"

Star paused momentarily and let her mind wonder back to her early childhood. "I want to help children who have lost their parents or have no shelter. I do not want any child to go without a loving family and a place to call home."

"That is what you will work on then. We have vast land around the palace where you can build a home for orphaned and homeless children. Have you and my son spoken of marriage as of yet?" the Queen questioned, intrigued to know the answer.

Star hesitated and shook her head, ever so slightly, as she looked down at the cup of tea in her clasp.

"Once the Battle of the Kingdoms is over, I am sure you

will have this talk," Queen Tee-Tee consoled Star.

"Your Highness, there is one thing that has been playing on my mind. I know that Prince Zaaki was protecting us when he killed my father and sister, but I cannot seem to stop thinking about it. It disturbs me, and it hurts," Star voiced as tears began to caress her cheeks.

Queen Tee-Tee held out her hand and placed it over Star's hand comfortingly.

"Star, you must look at it in the way it played out. It was the General and Sahara who attacked us. Zaaki only defended himself and us, and he had to do what he did so that we may live. If he did not defend us, we would not be here today. Please tell him how you feel, and you can work through this together. Now wipe those tears away and let us talk more about this home you want to build for children in need. It is a very admirable project, and I will be honoured to help you with getting it off the ground," Queen Tee-Tee said as she handed Star a napkin.

chapter Eleven
XI

Prince Zaaki went for a run before the wondrous flower of the sky had woken from her sleep and warmed the day ahead. He needed to escape all the troubles of the Kingdom, if only for an hour. He dressed in attire suitable for exercise and made his way outside. Running cleared his mind and allowed him to relax and release some tension. As he was running through the palace gardens, he saw a lady, dressed in Yistyyim's army uniform, going for a stroll and he bid her good morning.

"Good morning, Your Highness," she called out.

Prince Zaaki reached her side and asked her, "What is your name?"

"I am Sekhme, Your Highness," she courteously bowed her head down to him as she answered.

Prince Zaaki remained emotionless and nodded to her as he carried on running out of the gardens and into the fields beyond the Royal Palace. Prince Zaaki cleared his mind as he ran through the purple fields full of blossoming white and yellow exotic flowers. He passed through a forest of orange and red wild trees at the top of a hill. He gained speed as he began to run downhill. He felt exhilarated, and a sense of euphoria rushed through his body as he increased his speed even more. With the awakening of the sun above the horizon, Prince Zaaki knew that he had to make his way back to the palace. But first, he stopped to watch the most glorious sunrise in the distance. An overwhelming feeling of warmth and happiness came over him whilst he captured every minute of this splendid sight. After a few moments passed, he wiped the sweat off his forehead, took in a deep breath and launched into a sprint back to the palace.

Prince Zaaki arrived back home, sweating and out of breath. He ran up the stairs of the garden, and as he entered inside the palace, he bumped into Star, who was carrying a beautifully embroidered gold tray of breakfast to the Queen.

"I am terribly sorry, Star. Are you ok?" Prince Zaaki profusely apologized as he bent down to help her up.

"I am fine; spilled milk and breakfast can all be replaced. How was your run? I saw you leave at the break of dawn," Star said as she wiped the milk off her dress.

"Peaceful and energizing," he commented before carrying on. "I have missed you, Star. Please know you are in my heart always. I want to spend more time with you. I promise I will make time for us once the Battle of the Kingdoms is over. I have something important I want to ask you."

Star stared adoringly at Prince Zaaki as he placed his arms around her waist and pulled her closer to him. She wrapped her arms around him, and for that brief moment, all the worries of the world seemed to disappear. In that instant, in each other's embrace, all uncertainty and fear dissolved. Prince Zaaki felt calm and clear-headed, and Star felt his colossal undying love for her washing away all her hesitancies towards him. Their souls were connected and healed one another of pain, fear and confusion. Prince Zaaki was ready to fight for his Kingdom, for freedom and for peace.

"I must go now and get ready for the battle. Will you be with my parents on the Royal Balcony?" Prince Zaaki inquired.

"Yes, Your Highness, I will be with them. The Queen asked for only me to stand by her side during the battle. She told me that Protectius has requested that only the King, Queen, myself, Guardius and himself be in the Royal Balcony," Star reported.

"Very good," he responded.

"I better go and make another breakfast for Queen Tee-Tee. Good luck today, Zaaki, I will be there supporting you," she said as she carried the tray back to the kitchen.

Before the break of dawn, Zaeem arrived at the palace on horseback, hid his horse behind Strongheart in Strongheart's stall and made his way to Futuris' room in the basement, avoiding any servants and soldiers on duty. No one saw Zaeem as he safely entered Futuris' room where Futuris, Progra, Protectius, Guardius and King Zok awaited his presence.

"Finally! We can commence," Futuris sighed with relief.

Progra handed Protectius an unusual device that flickered a green light continuously, and he whispered, "Take this to Prince Zaaki. He knows what to do with it."

"If you all know what needs to be done here, I will go check on my army and make sure they all know their positions, before the battle starts," expressed Protectius as he slid the device under his navy-blue cloak.

"Yes, go. I have everything under control here. King Zok and Zaeem will be ready to leave in two hours. You can come back and escort them to the Royal Amphitheatre then," Futuris commanded.

"Very well," replied Protectius as he bowed down to King Zok and departed the room.

Sekhme quietly knocked on the door of Prince Yalem's suite and entered. She found Prince Yalem lying on his bed in a deep sleep and eerily watched him for a while. Slowly, he turned over from his left to right side in his sleep, which startled Sekhme. She took a step back, and her hand brushed against the vase of flowers on the table by the door. She used her magic to prevent it from hitting the ground and smashing to pieces, but the noise she made awoke Prince Yalem.

Prince Yalem opened his eyes and saw Sekhme standing by the door. "How long have you been standing there?"

"Not long, Prince Yalem," she said as she cleared her throat and
proceeded. "I wanted to let you know that I will be making my way now to the Royal Amphitheatre to release the potion on the army of men already there. They will be under your command once the battle commences. Is there anything else you require from me?"

"Sekhme, thank you for coming here and helping me on my quest to become the most powerful prince in all the kingdoms. One day, I shall rule all the kingdoms with you by my side."

chapter Twelve
XII

Crowds of excited and eager spectators arrived at the grand Royal Amphitheatre and made their way to their seats. Sunlight flowed into the Royal Amphitheatre and added warmth to the joyous occasion. The bold rays sauntered in, kindling shadows of orange and red amongst the spectators. They had come from all five of the Kingdoms to watch their prince or princess take part in this momentous battle for the newly found island.

The hostesses, wearing black tunics with the royal Luellan flag embroidered in silver thread on the top right of their uniforms, handed the audience leaflets as they entered. The leaflets written in exquisite calligraphy, explained the events of the day. The spectators, elated for the momentous day, wore their best attire and grins from ear to ear as they took to their seats with zeal.

Luella's Royal Amphitheatre presents
The Battle of The Kingdoms

Kingdoms	Contestants	Judges
Kingdom of Luella	Prince Zaaki	Aadeh
Kingdom of Yistyyim	Prince Yalem	Jugor
Kingdom of Sorreno	Princess Joula	Domero
Kingdom of Tranquily	Princess Teensy	Taress
Kingdom of Roderna	Prince Rousse	Kastis

Four Rounds in The Battle of The Kingdoms

Round 1	Battle of Cause and Effect	Blue and White Room
Round 2	Battle of the Word	Yellow Room
Round 3	Battle of the Soul	Red Room
Round 4	Battle of the Mind	Green Room

A member of the Royal Band of Luella started to play a fanfare trumpet, and the spectators went silent. The Royal Band all joined in and played their instruments as they marched out onto the stage, led by the lead trumpeter. The forty members of the Royal Band wore olive green trouser suits and berets as they marched into the center of the Amphitheatre Stage, playing the Royal Anthem of the Kingdom of Luella. There were two band members waving the Kingdom of Luella's flag on either side of the band.

Once it was finished, the spectators' eyes moved to the Royal Balcony where the King and Queen of Luella were standing. King Zok and Queen Tee-Tee gave a royal wave to the spectators before sitting down in their regal seats. Protectius and Guardius stood behind the King, and Star, with two Luellan soldiers, stood behind Queen Tee-Tee. As soon as they were comfortably seated, the crowd applauded and hailed the King of Luella. The applause filled the Royal Amphitheatre as the five judges took to the stage. The judges stood on a swiveling rose gold podium so that the judges addressed the whole crowd of spectators circling them.

The head judge was Aadeh from the Kingdom of Luella, the second judge was Jugor from the Kingdom of Yistyyim, the third judge was Domero from the Kingdom of Sorreno, the fourth judge was Taress from the Kingdom of Tranquily and the fifth and final judge was Kastis from the Kingdom of Roderna. All five judges wore burgundy gowns and wigs to distinguish themselves as impartial and to draw on the supremacy of the law.

"Welcome to the momentous Battle of the Kingdoms,

here at the Royal Amphitheatre in the Kingdom of Luella," exclaimed Judge Aadeh.

Jugor followed, "We are pleased to announce that Prince Zaaki will be representing the Kingdom of Luella."

Prince Zaaki walked onto the stage of the Amphitheatre and began to walk around the edges of the stage, waving at the crowds of people. He saw Star in the Royal Balcony and blew her a kiss.

Jugor continued, "Prince Yalem will be representing the Kingdom of Yistyyim."

Prince Yalem boldly walked onto the stage with a smug grin as he joined Prince Zaaki, walking around the outskirts of the stage, greeting all the spectators. Prince Yalem was overwrought with anticipation as his plan was about to unfold on this special day. The thought of taking over the Kingdom of Luella and maliciously killing Prince Zaaki and King Zok permeated his mind as he callously waved at the spectators.

Jugor diplomatically introduced the remaining contestants. Princess Joula, representing the Kingdom of Sorreno, walked onto the stage, oozing confidence and beauty, with her long black hair neatly braided in two braids. She proudly joined Prince Yalem and Prince Zaaki as they welcomed the audience. Princess Teensy, usually displaying a cheerful and bubbly nature, was on edge with nervousness as she stumbled onto the stage after her name was announced. She fumbled her way towards the three contestants on the stage and joined them in acknowledging the spectators. Princess Teensy was representing the Kingdom of Tranquily. Prince Rousse from the Kingdom of Roderna, a lanky young man with a pale complexion, arrogantly marched onto the stage with a swagger as soon as he heard his name.

The contestants all wore glistening fitted silver battle suits with their names embroidered in thick black thread on the back of their tops.

"There are four rounds in the Battle of the Kingdoms, and they will take place in four different rooms that will appear on this very stage. The first round is called the Battle of Cause and Effect, taking place in the blue and white room. You will see five doors of entry into each room. The contestants will each enter from their own door," explained Aadeh.

Once Aadeh stopped talking, the Royal Band took their cue to exit the stage, marching and still playing the national anthem of Luella. The judges stepped off the podium and walked to the side of the stage. Magically the stage flipped one hundred and eighty degrees and a pentagonal blue and white room emerged. The five shiny black doors, on each vertex of the pentagon, were engraved with the contestants' names.

"Now, contestants, please go to your assigned doors! Whatever happens once the battle has started, you must endeavour to continue onto the next round or forfeit your place in the battle. The one who completes all four rounds successfully will be hailed the winner! One player will be eliminated in each round," Aadeh commanded, then proceeded to explain round one. "Once you hear the bell, you may use one spell. Use it wisely to get through the maze of jeopardy, safely. Act with confidence, foresee the consequences, but beware of ignorance."

The five judges took their places around the pentagonal blue and white room. The head judge, Aadeh, stood by a large brass bell hanging from a black wooden stand. He waited for silence throughout the majestic Royal Amphitheatre. The spectators anxiously leant forward in their seats, their eyes glued on the blue and white room that appeared around the center stage of the Amphitheatre.

"Without further ado, let the Battle of the Kingdoms commence!" Aadeh announced, and he rang the bell.

Prince Zaaki, Prince Yalem, Princess Teensy, Princess Joula and Prince Rousse all opened their respective doors and entered the blue and white room. The participants of the battle saw an empty room with blue walls, a white floor, and a white ceiling. From the viewpoint of the spectators, the walls and ceilings were transparent so that they could clearly watch the contestants' every action. Prince Zaaki noticed Princess Teensy opposite him, at the other end of the room, and glanced around to see the other contestants scattered around the room. The doors behind the participants closed shut and vanished, with the room magically transforming into an unusual looking maze with constantly sliding blue walls. Not only the walls, but also parts of the floor beneath them, were constantly sliding to reveal holes into darkness and failure. One wrong move and someone would literally fall out of the battle and leave the competition. The contestants had to make their way through the maze and find the exit into the next round. Their actions would dictate their place in the battle.

Prince Zaaki stood still, watching the walls and floor sliding in and out, and calculated his next move. He knew he could use one spell to help him within this round, but he also knew that he might need the spell later on, hence when he saw the floor and walls aligned to show him a clear pathway into the next part of the maze, he took it. Cautiously, he took his first steps and stopped once he reached a hole in the ground. He looked down and saw an endless darkness. Quickly, the walls shifted again, and he continued to make his way through the maze, consistently calculating his next moves. The other contestants did the same, carefully making their way through this ever-changing maze. All the contestants reached a point where they had to choose between three paths. The three paths looked identical.

Prince Zaaki began to recite a spell, "Rid the two paths of failure and show me the true path to lead me out of this maze and into round two of the battle."

Prince Zaaki:
Sheel ill galat ou khale bas ill masbout Khidne alla aljawlat thania

With the last word of his spell, all three paths flickered until two disintegrated, and Prince Zaaki made his way through the remaining path. He successfully completed the first round and opened the door that appeared in front of him. He exited round one and found himself standing in the corner of the Amphitheatre waiting for his fellow competitors to also complete round one.

Almost immediately after Prince Zaaki, Prince Yalem and Princess Teensy successfully completed the first round. They found themselves standing in their starting places once again. They all waited in anticipation to see who would be the next to make it through, Princess Joula or Prince Rousse. Time was passing by, and everyone watched as Princess Joula and Prince Rousse tried to manoeuvre through the maze. Suddenly Prince Rousse made a wrong turn and fell into a dark hole. He had failed and was out of the battle. Princess Joula, unaware of what was happening with the other contestants, persisted and finally used a spell that allowed her to successfully enter into the second round.

The Kingdom of Roderna was eliminated from the Battle of the Kingdoms.

chapter Thirteen
XIII

Aadeh appeared on the stage and announced, "Firstly, let us bid farewell to Prince Rousse."

The audience clapped and hailed Prince Rousse as he reappeared on the stage and waved farewell to the spectators.

Aadeh continued, "Now, congratulations to Prince Zaaki, Prince Yalem, Princess Teensy and Princess Joula. You are about to enter round two, the Battle of the Word. Please take a step back, and the yellow room will materialize."

The ground swiveled a hundred and eighty degrees yet again, and as the blue and white room disappeared beneath the ground, the yellow room emerged.

Aadeh announced, "To seek the truth and continue in the battle, find the words you will need within this room of troubles. Use these words within your actions. Again, a spell may be used to aid you in completing this round successfully. I will ask you one question before you enter the battle of the word; are you four remaining contestants friend or foe?" Aadeh raised his hand and rang the brass bell for the second time.

The remaining four contestants entered through their respective doors into the square yellow room and found themselves in a continually spinning room, spinning on its axis. Words appeared, vanished and reappeared on the walls and ceiling with the blink of an eye. One. Spirit. Protect. Power. Love. Unite. Fight. Strength. Desire. Reason. Knowledge. Win. Success. Great. Defend. Attack. Soul. Kindness. As the contestants were looking for the exit into round three, the room stopped spinning and a game on the floor materialised. It was a large square with a diagonal path from each vertex of the square. The outskirts of the path floor vanished, and a deep pit of darkness was seen. On this path were three square shaped steps, each blocked by a transparent wall. The contestants realized that they needed to make their way to the center of the square to get through to the next round. For the wall to come down, the contestants were required to find the correct word so that they may proceed.

Domero voiced the first clue, "The history of the Kingdoms."

The four contestants stared at the words visualizing for only a second in front of them and chose accordingly.

They all chose Knowledge. As soon as they did, the

respective walls slowly dissolved, and they moved forward into the next section. Another transparent wall stood before them.

Domero said, "The battle of your sword comes into play."

Out of nowhere, flying red fireballs viciously attacked the contestants. They all drew their swords and hit the fireballs away from their bodies.

"Everyone, defend yourselves!" Prince Zaaki shouted out to the other contestants.

The wall in front of Prince Zaaki dissolved and he escaped the wrath of the fireballs. He was in the final section of this round.

It took the other three contestants a while to figure out that the word was 'defend,' and they moved into the next section of the round.

Domero informed the four contestants that this final section would only allow the first three contestants through to the next round. He followed by repeating, "Friend or foe?"

The four contestants could see each other through the transparent walls. Words continued to visualize and disappear all around them.

Without warning, a flock of dragons entered the yellow room and headed straight for Prince Zaaki.

Princess Teensy screamed, "Prince Zaaki, behind you!"

Prince Zaaki turned around and saw ten Sanquito Dragons hurdling towards him. He was expecting them, so he was prepared to defend himself. Prince Zaaki stabbed the first Sanquito Dragon in its heart, and it fell to its death in the pit of darkness adjacent to the step Prince Zaaki was standing on. The Sanquito Dragons flapped their bat-like wings as they attacked Prince Zaaki. He stabbed another dragon and killed it but struggled to fight the remaining dragons alone.

Hence, he raised his sword to his eye level and recited a spell in Libnene, "Unite the strength of the contestants to fight the dragons."

Prince Zaaki:
Tawhid quaate almutasabin limuharabat altananin

Princess Teensy repeated the spell and found herself transported to Prince Zaaki's side. She fought the Sanquito Dragons alongside Prince Zaaki. Prince Yalem watched, hoping that one of the dragons would successfully kill Prince Zaaki. After a while, Prince Yalem realized that to win this round, they all needed to come together, hence reluctantly repeated the spell Prince Zaaki said. He was transported to Princess Teensy and Prince Zaaki's side. Princess Joula saw what was happening but decided to try and find the word to move her into the next round successfully.

"Win!" Princess Joula shouted; all of a sudden, the floor beneath her gave way, and she fell into the pit of darkness, instantly eliminated from the battle.

The remaining three, together, fought the Sanquito Dragons, all the while struggling to catch their breath. Prince Zaaki somersaulted over one of the dragons, landing on its back. Then, with one swift motion of his sword, he cut the dragon's head off. The dragon fell into the pit of darkness. Without hesitation, Prince Zaaki jumped and landed safely on the path. Princess Teensy pierced her sword through one of the dragon's hearts. Prince Yalem acted as if he was helping, but in reality, he was not doing much to defend the other two.

As soon as all the Sanquito Dragons in the yellow room were killed, the wall dissolved in front of Prince Zaaki, Princess Teensy and Prince Yalem, standing side-by-side. Together, they walked forward into the center of the square. Unexpectedly, the yellow room magically disintegrated. The remaining three contestants stood in the middle of the stage gazing out into the crowd of spectators applauding and hailing them.

Prince Zaaki turned his gaze to the Royal Balcony and in the distance saw something flying towards the Amphitheatre. He looked harder and realized that General Scarytis was riding on the back of a Sanquito Dragon. He also saw a woman riding on the back of another Sanquito Dragon. General Scarytis was leading swarms of Sanquito Dragons towards the Amphitheatre.

Protectius and Guardius saw the dragons and drew their swords, ready to defend the King and Queen of Luella. Star held the Queen's hand tightly as they knew they were about to be attacked. Protectius handed Star a sword and told her to use it to defend Queen Tee-Tee.

Prince Zaaki knew he had to use the spell Futuris had given him to freeze everyone in the Royal Amphitheatre, with the exception of those in the Royal Balcony. Without further ado, he recited the spell and then beckoned Strongheart.

Prince Zaaki:
Jamad aljamie bas mis ill
fi shurfat almalakia

In a flurry of beating wings, Strongheart flew to Prince Zaaki. Prince Zaaki mounted Strongheart and they made their way to the Royal Balcony. While the spectators were all frozen in their seats, Prince Zaaki knew he only had five minutes until the spell would wear off. Unfortunately, the spell was not strong enough to work on General Scarytis and the Sanquito Dragons, and they headed straight for King Zok.

General Scarytis ordered the Sanquito Dragons, "Go to the King and Queen in the Royal Balcony!"

The Sanquito Dragons flew straight into the protective shield surrounding the Royal Balcony and bounced backwards. The woman riding on the back of one of the dragons by the General's side, the General's witch Ugat, raised her right hand and pointed her index finger at the protective shield.

"Remove this shield from my path. Burn it to the ground!" Ugat exclaimed as she used her powers of witchery to burn the protective shield. Unlike Sekhme, a wizardess who creates potions and spells, Ugat was a witch born with powers.

Strongheart flew up behind General Scarytis, and Prince Zaaki sliced a piece of the Sanquito Dragon's wing that was carrying the General. Swiftly, Prince Zaaki jumped off Strongheart's back and landed in the Royal Balcony. General Scarytis followed and jumped off the injured Sanquito Dragon. They began to clash swords and dueled fervently. Protectius and Guardius impressively battled the Sanquito Dragons two at a time.

Ugat used her powers to transport herself to King Zok's side. She grabbed him and covered him with her long black cloak. In a flash, they both vanished into thin air.

"She took King Zok! Zaaki, she took your father!" Queen Tee-Tee bellowed.

Protectius called out as he was fighting off the dragons, "Do not worry, Your Majesty! We will get him back!"

One of the Sanquito Dragons attacked Star and the Queen. Ardently, Star attacked the dragon. She swished the sword from side to side, luckily cutting the dragon's wing.

"Stab it in the heart! And stay clear of its mouth," called out Prince Zaaki.

"Ok, I will try!" a panicked Star shouted out.

She took her sword, and with one solid motion pierced

the heart of the dragon. It fell onto the ground in front of Star and the Queen, spewing out grey blood.

"Star, well done!" exhaled a very relieved Queen Tee-Tee.

Star, feeling empowered that she defended Queen Tee-Tee successfully, continued to fight off other Sanquito Dragons. This time she yielded the sword with even more intense fierceness and boldness.

Guardius and Protectius fought all the dragons with the surprising help of Star. Prince Zaaki fought the General until he had him pinned on the ground. Prince Zaaki pierced his sword through General Scarytis' armour but stopped. He did not want to kill him this time.

"Guardius, take him away. I will deal with him later," Prince Zaaki commanded.

Guardius took the General down into the basement of the Amphitheatre where they had built a special prison for the evil General.

Queen Tee-Tee sobbed and broke down in tears, "Zaaki, your father. Please, please go find him. That woman, that evil witch, took him."

"Mother, calm down. That was not Father. Father is safe. Please do not worry," Prince Zaaki said reassuringly.

"What do you mean that was not your father?"

"Zaeem took his place. We have been preparing for this

attack and knew that Father's life would be threatened, thus Zaeem offered to take his identity during the Battle of the Kingdoms. Rest assured; Father is safe. And Zaeem knows what to do. I must return to the stage and resume my position before the spell wears off the spectators and judges," said Prince Zaaki as he jumped onto Strongheart, who was hovering in mid-air in front of the Royal Balcony.

Strongheart flew Prince Zaaki to the middle of the stage, swiftly departing just as the spell wore off, and the spectators continued to applaud the remaining three contestants.

Ugat reappeared in a field near the Royal Amphitheatre and removed the cloak covering the impersonator.

"You are not the King!" said Ugat angrily.

"No!" Zaeem replied, and he drew his sword at her throat.

"It is not wise to kill a witch. I will haunt you forever," threatened Ugat.

"You do not scare me, witch," Zaeem laughed as he dug his sword deep into her throat.

She grabbed his arm with her left hand; her nails pierced through his shirt and sank into his skin. Zaeem dug his sword deeper into her throat, until he could see it piercing through the other side of her neck, blood violently spewing out of her throat. Her nails scraped down his arm as she fell to the ground and to her ultimate death. Zaeem removed his sword from her throat and noticed his arm was bleeding. He quickly tore off a piece of his clothing and wrapped it around his wound before he hurried back to the Royal Amphitheatre.

chapter Fourteen
XIV

Prince Zaaki rushed to Aadeh and whispered, "Please, calmly tell the audience that was part of the event, then proceed with the Battle as we have no choice but to continue."

Aadeh nervously announced, "We hope you enjoyed the show we put on for you with the dragons. Now, let us all bid farewell to Princess Joula from the Kingdom of Sorreno," he paused to allow the spectators to applaud Princess Joula before continuing. "Please congratulate Princess Teensy, Prince Zaaki and Prince Yalem in getting through to the next round. Judge Kastis will now explain round three."

Kastis announced, "Round three is the Battle of the Soul, which will take place in the triangular red room. Please take your places, contestants."

The final three contestants took their places as the floor

of the stage opened, and the red room appeared from below the ground. Once the red room had magically risen, Kastis further explained, "This may look like a simple round, for it is a race to reach the exit, but the race path is not what it seems. You will meet your deepest desire within. Will you be tempted or not? Decide your fate within this triangle. Once the bell is rung, you may enter."

The crowd quietened down, intrigued and anxious to see what was in store for the contestants in this room. Aadeh rang the brass bell.

The three remaining contestants entered the triangular red room and found themselves standing alone, surrounded by red walls, a red ceiling and a red floor. They eagerly waited for the race path to visualize. Suddenly, the rooms they were in started to move. Prince Zaaki's room began to move upwards, and Princess Teensy's room began to move downwards. The triangular rooms shifted to align one above the other in a tiered format. The walls separating them disappeared into thin air and a racetrack visualized. Hastily, they all bolted as fast they could. They all ran into the redness, with no end in sight.

"Teensy, slow down and wait for me," Prince Zaaki beckoned to Princess Teensy.

Princess Teensy did as Prince Zaaki asked of her and slowed down, coming to a dead stop. Prince Zaaki held out his hands and Princess Teensy held on to them, taken aback by his beautiful green-blue eyes.

"Do you want to be with me?" asked Prince Zaaki, as he let go of her hand and affectionately brushed a strand of her hair from her face.

"Yes, yes I do," replied a very impatient Princess Teensy.

Princess Teensy just stood in the middle of round three, mesmerized by Prince Zaaki's eyes, blissfully unaware that this was all in her head. She had imagined her deepest desire and she was drawn into her own illusion. Oblivious to her actions, she had forfeited the battle.

All the while Prince Yalem and Prince Zaaki were trying to fight their deepest desires within their minds as they continued to run.

Prince Yalem succumbed to his deepest desire of ruling the Kingdom of Luella at the cost of killing King Zok and Prince Zaaki. He saw himself drive a dagger through King Zok's chest as Sekhme held Prince Zaaki down with a spell, forcing him to watch his father be brutally murdered by Prince Yalem. Prince Yalem, enticed by this desire, resisted temptation to continue it and resumed to play in the race.

Prince Zaaki desperately tried to resist his deepest desire, which was to wed Star and share a happy life with her. He briefly imagined his future with Star and their unborn children running around the palace gardens, playing with the Girtigs and Zebflas, just as he did when he was a child. Prince Zaaki resolutely resisted his deepest desire and ran as fast as he could, not tempted in the slightest to look back at the other contestants. Finally, he saw the end and dashed towards it. He had successfully exited round three and came to a stop outside the red room.

Not more than two minutes later, Prince Yalem came speeding out of the red room. Abruptly, the red room lowered into the ground and out of sight. The audience loudly applauded the two finalists, Prince Zaaki and Prince Yalem.

Aadeh announced, "Princess Teensy, unfortunately, fell for temptation and is eliminated. Our finalists are Prince Yalem and Prince Zaaki. Please take your places. Taress will explain the fourth and final round."

Zaeem arrived back at the Royal Amphitheatre and made his way up to the Royal Balcony. Two rows below the Royal Balcony sat King Zok in disguise. He saw Zaeem and stood up and walked towards him.

"Zaeem, I will go resume my seat with my wife now in the Royal Balcony. Thank you for taking my place, but I cannot sit idly by any longer and watch all of you under attack and do nothing," King Zok ordered under his breath.

"King Zok, with all due respect, this is not over. There is still another attack looming, and this is the one we are unsure of," petitioned Zaeem with caution.

"I have faith in my son, you, Protectius and the Luellan

army. Take me to the Royal Balcony. And that is an order!" firmly instructed a very stubborn King Zok.

"Very well, Your Majesty," Zaeem reluctantly complied as they both made their way to Queen Tee-Tee in the Royal Balcony.

Once they arrived, Queen Tee-Tee jumped from her seat and warmly embraced her husband. Protectius, noticing Zaeem's arm was bleeding profusely, asked him how he was injured.

"It's just a scratch," Zaeem insisted.

Zaeem was a strong man with a feeling of invincibility about him. He exuded a confidence in his strength, health and mortality that was inspiring. Zaeem knew it would take more than a silly old witch to knock him down.

"This is not just a scratch, Zaeem. There is too much blood. Tell me this is not from the witch?" Protectius asked anxiously.

Zaeem was Protectius' teacher and mentor, and he had a duty of care towards Zaeem. Protectius' nature was to protect and serve, but for Zaeem it was more so. Protectius saw Zaeem as a father figure.

"Yes, it is from her nails. She grabbed hold of me as I stabbed my sword in her throat. Why?" Zaeem curiously questioned.

"A witch's nails are poisonous. When she pierced her

nails into your skin, she poisoned you. We have no time to lose. Guardius, you need to get Zaeem to Futuris at the Royal Palace, posthaste. He will know what to do." Protectius declared, impatiently.

Zaeem tried to resist, insisting that the King needed his service imminently and that he would go to Futuris after the Battle of the Kingdoms had finished. But Protectius persisted and finally, Zaeem agreed; Guardius accompanied Zaeem towards the stables of the Royal Amphitheatre to fetch their horses and ride to the Royal Palace.

Goddess Ella and Goddess Lulu sat amongst the spectators in the Royal Amphitheatre incognito, accompanied by Jamilietta, Panacea, Fred, Baal, Karena and Immanuel. The Goddesses were aware of everything that had happened and quietly ordered Jamilietta to transport Panacea to the stables where she could heal Zaeem.

chapter Fifteen
XV

Taress explained, "Round four is the Battle of the Mind. It will take place in the circular green room. Prince Yalem and Prince Zaaki, you will go head-to-head in this final round. To win the battle, you must overcome the hallucinogenic images before you. Your mind will need to distinguish reality from illusion. Beware of your mind, it will play tricks on you. When you hear the bell, you may enter. Good luck to you both."

Aadeh rang the brass bell, and the two princes opened their respective doors leading into the circular green room. Instantly, Prince Zaaki and Prince Yalem stood at opposite sides of the green room and saw both King Zok and King Salem appear in the middle. The King of Yistyyim held a sword in his hand, ready to attack Prince Zaaki, while at the same time King Zok drew his sword to attack Prince Yalem. Whilst Prince Yalem entered into a duel with King Zok, fiercely trying to kill King Zok, Prince Zaaki was only defending himself against the King of Yistyyim's brutal attack.

Prince Zaaki, distracted by Prince Yalem and his father engaged in an intense sword fight, thought of a way to go to his father's aid. Advertently, Prince Zaaki escaped the King of Yistyyim's attack, with a somersault over his head, and rushed to help King Zok. Prince Zaaki pushed King Zok out of the line of fire and entered into a heated sword fight with Prince Yalem. As the two Princes continued to battle, both Kings disappeared from the green room. Prince Yalem savagely stabbed Prince Zaaki's right shoulder. Thus, Prince Zaaki threw his sword into his left hand and resumed attack on Prince Yalem. As he somersaulted over Prince Yalem, he slit Prince Yalem's sleeve, not wounding his wrist. They dueled until Star appeared in the middle of the green room. Prince Yalem rushed to Star and forcefully pulled her body towards his as he placed his sword against her throat.

"No! Let her go!" yelled Prince Zaaki.

"Forfeit the Battle of the Kingdoms, and I will!" demanded Prince Yalem.

"Never!" Prince Zaaki called out.

"Then watch her die," sniggered Prince Yalem as his sword began to go deeper into Star's throat.

Prince Zaaki ran towards them and leaped over Star and Prince Yalem. Landing crouched down behind Prince Yalem, without hesitation, Prince Zaaki swung his sword across Prince Yalem's right leg. Prince Yalem let go of Star and grabbed his injured leg.

"Star, run!" hollered Prince Zaaki.

Suddenly, Star vanished into thin air and Prince Yalem fell to the ground. The back of his leg was seriously wounded and bleeding. He ripped one of the sleeves of his shirt and bandaged it tightly to stop blood from escaping. Prince Yalem proceeded to attack Prince Zaaki.

"Have you not had enough?" asked Prince Zaaki.

"No! I will win this battle! I will rule your Kingdom, and if I have to kill you to do that, then so be it!" Prince Yalem proclaimed.

"You will never rule my Kingdom!" Prince Zaaki countered as he clashed swords with Prince Yalem.

Furious, Prince Yalem called out to Sekhme before he raised his left wrist and ordered the Yistyyim and Luellan army to attack King Zok, through his CB.

"What did you do?" Prince Zaaki shouted.

Suddenly, four Prince Yalems materialised standing next to the real Prince Yalem, and four Prince Zaakis materialized standing adjacent to Prince Zaaki. All the Prince Yalem doubles began to fight all but one of the Prince Zaaki doubles. One of the Prince Zaakis closed his eyes and used the power of his mind to distinguish between real and imaginary. His mind cleared, and he focused on the one real Prince Yalem. Prince Zaaki singled him out and pushed all the imaginary doubles out of his way. Prince Zaaki vehemently clashed his sword against Prince Yalem's sword, throwing the sword across the room. Prince Yalem tried to run towards his sword but tripped and fell. Prince Zaaki stood over Prince Yalem with his sword over his chest.

All of a sudden, the room vanished with the imaginary Princes, and Prince Zaaki looked around to see the mayhem within the Amphitheatre.

"You will never defeat me!" hailed Prince Yalem as he saw his sword lying on the ground behind Prince Zaaki.

Prince Zaaki beckoned Strongheart, and in the blink of an eye Strongheart swiftly flew to Prince Zaaki. As Prince Zaaki mounted Strongheart, Prince Yalem rushed to grab his sword and took a final swing at Prince Zaaki. He stabbed through Prince Zaaki's jacket as Strongheart flew Prince Zaaki towards the Royal Balcony.

"Did he get you? Are you ok, Your Highness?" asked Strongheart worriedly.

Prince Zaaki put his hand to his chest and felt the hole in his jacket but didn't see or feel any blood. Then he searched the inside of his jacket pocket to find the compass Star had given him was ever so slightly dented. It had saved his life, halting the sword from stabbing him in his heart.

"I am lucky, Strongheart. I am a very lucky man to have Star love me," Prince Zaaki chuckled before continuing, "I'm not injured. Anyway, where are they?" Prince Zaaki frantically said as they flew past the deserted balcony.

"I do not know, Your Highness. We will find them," Strongheart murmured, trying to reassure Prince Zaaki.

"Why is our army attacking the spectators? Where is Protectius?" Prince Zaaki cried out in absolute shock.

"Prince Zaaki, over here!" Baal shouted out, standing up and waving at Strongheart and Prince Zaaki.

"Go, Strongheart, over there to Baal. The Goddesses are with him!" ordered Prince Zaaki.

Hastily, Strongheart flew up the tiered seats of the Royal Amphitheatre towards Baal.

Prince Zaaki called out, "Goddess Ella, what is going on? Why is everyone fighting? And I cannot find my parents or Star or Protectius. They seem to have vanished from the Royal Balcony!"

"Prince Yalem is controlling the army. He has put some kind of spell over them. I have seen this before. This is the work of an evil wizardess, Sekhme. You have something with you that I believe can help," Goddess Ella spoke softly and calmly even though there was absolute chaos around her.

"Yes, yes, Progra made this and said I would know when it would be needed."

"Hand it to Baal. Baal will deal with the Luellan and Yistyyim armies and anyone else infected. You must take Karena with you and find your parents. She can heal them if they are injured. Fred will take Immanuel to help the injured spectators," Goddess Ella gracefully commanded. Prince Zaaki took something from his pocket and handed it to Baal.

Goddess Lulu interrupted, "Before you go Prince Zaaki, I will locate Sekhme."

Goddess Lulu took off the hood and cloak masking her identity and began to float in mid-air. A silver beam of light circled her body as a white cloud formed beneath her feet and raised her into the sky, high above the Royal Amphitheatre. She spun around and around before coming down.

"Sekhme is dead. Charon is awaiting her soul. Some of the Yistyyim soldiers have taken your parents, Star and Protectius. I can see Protectius, and he is unconscious. They are headed out of the grounds of the Amphitheatre over there." Goddess Lulu pointed in the direction to the north of the Royal Amphitheatre.

Without delay, Prince Zaaki helped Karena mount Strongheart and they flew towards them.

"Baal, you know what you must do now," Goddess Lulu ordered.

Baal held out the device in his hands and focused on his powers. Suddenly, an electric silver-white glow encompassed his whole body, elevating it off the ground. Baal, God-like with his extraordinary power, turned the sky dark and eerie before creating a colossal

thunderstorm, which attacked the whole Kingdom of Luella. The device in Baal's hands elevated and became part of the storm. Electric blue rain fell down onto everyone in the Kingdom of Luella, beginning to wash away the evil potion controlling the minds of those infected by Sekhme. The menacing thunder echoed throughout the Royal Amphitheatre. Baal looked down and saw Prince Zaaki in battle with Prince Yalem and ten soldiers. He scanned the field to the north of the Royal Amphitheatre for Karena but could not see her. He raged with anger and let out lightning bolts from his eyes onto Prince Yalem and his men, trying to avoid Prince Zaaki. Successfully, he struck some of the soldiers. Then his eyes clocked Karena kneeling by Protectius' side, healing him.

As the electric blue rain continued to fall, the soldiers infected with Sekhme's poison began to stop attacking the innocent spectators. They looked confused, dropped their weapons and let go of people they were attacking.

Prince Yalem saw his men drop their swords and halt the attack on the Royal family of Luella. He started yelling, "What are you doing? Fight them! Help me, you imbeciles!"

Prince Zaaki continued to clash swords with his vehement opponent, Prince Yalem. Prince Yalem, enraged at his men, was slightly distracted by what was happening to them.

Prince Zaaki took his opportunity and struck Prince Yalem with his sword across the cheek and hailed, "It's over, Yalem. You have lost. You will always lose to us.

Evil has no place here!"

Prince Yalem incensed, monstrously dueled with Prince Zaaki, "Never! I will win! I will rule your Kingdom!"

Prince Yalem channeled all his energy to fight Prince Zaaki and swung the blade with all his might against Prince Zaaki's sword. Prince Zaaki's sword flew out of his hand and landed near Karena and Protectius.

"Protectius, please, please, get up! You are healed. Prince Zaaki needs you!" Karena begged Protectius.

Prince Yalem pinned Prince Zaaki to the ground with his sword over his chest.

Protectius opened his eyes and lifted himself off the ground. He picked up Prince Zaaki's sword and rushed to Prince Zaaki's aid.

Protectius took a mighty leap and landed behind Prince Yalem.

"Let go of the sword or I will strike your heart!" Protectius threatened Prince Yalem.

"I will not die in vain. I will take you with me, Prince Zaaki!" Prince Yalem shouted as he ran his sword through Prince Zaaki's chest.

Protectius killed Prince Yalem, brazenly, with one clean strike of his sword, piercing through his chest and into his heart.

"Prince Zaaki!" yelled Protectius.

Star ran towards Prince Zaaki, who was lying on the ground, struggling to breathe. "Zaaki! Zaaki! No!"

Karena ran over towards Prince Zaaki and tried to heal his wound. Her powers were not strong enough.

"Star, where are the King and Queen?" Prince Zaaki desperately asked, taking a deep breath with every word.

"Some soldiers took King Zok and Queen Tee-Tee ahead of us. King Zok was injured because he tried to fight the soldiers. Queen Tee-Tee managed to stop the bleeding by ripping her dress and bandaging his leg. I sent Strongheart to find them and bring them here," Star informed him as she wiped the tears from her eyes and cheeks.

"This wound is too deep. I cannot heal it," Karena wept uncontrollably.

"Karena, the Goddesses told me that you have extraordinary gifts. I know you can do this. Focus, please," Prince Zaaki encouraged Karena as he fought for breath.

Prince Zaaki fell unconscious and Star screamed out his name.

Suddenly, Fred appeared with Immanuel, who knelt down by Karena's side. Karena and Immanuel both placed their hands over Prince Zaaki's wounded chest. Red and orange electric currents visualized between their hands and Prince Zaaki's body. Protectius tried to hide his tears as he caught Fred staring at him.

"Please save him! Please!" Star cried out to Karena and Immanuel.

Goddess Lulu and Goddess Ella magically appeared in the sky, directly above Prince Zaaki. The thunderstorm disappeared and the Goddesses majestically raised Prince Zaaki's body above the ground. As his body floated in mid-air, he began to wake. His wound healed and he stood up. The Goddesses slowly brought him back to the ground and Star embraced Prince Zaaki tightly.

"Karena and Immanuel, your powers are becoming stronger. You saved Prince Zaaki today. Believe in yourselves and your powers. When you unite, your powers are stronger. A valuable lesson has been taught here," Goddess Ella said before continuing, "Fred, take Immanuel and go help Baal. He is rescuing the people in the Amphitheatre. Karena, you will come with us, as Charon is in need of your assistance."

"Protectius, we must go find my parents!" Prince Zaaki insisted as he let go of Star's embrace.

"No need. Look over there, I see them with Strongheart," Protectius replied with relief.

Prince Zaaki ran towards Strongheart as he landed a few meters away. He helped Queen Tee-Tee dismount Strongheart and then carried King Zok off Strongheart and laid him on the ground.

"Father, what happened?" Prince Zaaki asked worriedly.

"I am fine, a small cut on my leg. Your mother dealt with it," King Zok reassured his son.

King Zok saw Protectius standing adjacent to Prince Zaaki and asked him to fetch the Royal Carriage to take them back to the Royal Palace.

Hysterically, Queen Tee-Tee interrupted King Zok. "What if we are attacked again? Protectius and Prince Zaaki should stay with us, dear. You are injured and cannot stand on your leg, let alone walk."

"It is nothing, my love, really. The Royal Physician will tend to my wound back at the palace," insisted King Zok.

"Mother, you are safe now. We put a stop to Prince Yalem and General Scarytis. Father, are you sure?" Prince Zaaki inquired.

"Yes. Protectius, please go now and fetch the carriage," King Zok instructed.

"Take Strongheart. We will be fine here," Prince Zaaki said as he held his mother's hand.

Following the King's orders, Protectius mounted Strongheart and flew to the stables at the Royal Amphitheatre, posthaste.

chapter Sixteen
XVI

Strongheart and Protectius arrived at the stables of the Royal Amphitheatre. Protectius called out to three Luellan soldiers in the near distance and ordered them to take the Royal Carriage and follow Strongheart, at once, to King Zok and Queen Tee-Tee. The soldiers quickly made their way to the Royal Carriage and followed Strongheart out of the stables. Protectius watched them depart and breathed out a deep sigh of relief. As he was about to make his way into the Amphitheatre to find Zaeem and Guardius, he heard voices coming from one of the stalls in the stables, hence he walked towards the stall. As soon as he peered in the stall, he saw Guardius lying on the ground with his head propped up on a woman's lap. Zaeem and another woman were kneeling by Guardius, both with tears rolling down their faces.

Protectius hurried into the stall, fell to his knees by Guardius' side and cried out, "What happened?"

"We were taken by surprise. The Luellan army with a wizardess attacked us as we were mounting our horses. Guardius was struck and fell of his horse. But he picked himself up and fought this wizardess and killed her as I fought the Luellan army soldiers. I caught a glimpse of this wizardess blow a potion of some sort into Guardius' face just before he slit her throat and she bled to death. He fell to the ground and stopped breathing." Zaeem wiped away the tears streaming down his face. "Then out of the blue, a lady, Panacea, appeared from out of nowhere with Jamilietta to help me. She healed my wound, but it was too late for Guardius," a heartbroken Zaeem explained as he held Guardius' cold hand, weeping.

In absolute shock, Protectius locked eyes with his past, the love of his life who had disappeared many years ago without a trace.

Jamilietta stared into his eyes and said, "I am so sorry, Protectius. We tried to save him. The soldiers grabbed Panacea and myself. Zaeem intervened and fought them, but it was too late for Panacea to heal him."

"What do you mean heal him? Panacea, how is that possible?" Protectius asked, trying to avoid the questions racing in his mind that he wanted to ask Jamilietta.

Panacea replied, trying to hold back her weeping, "I have a gift and can heal people, but I wasn't able to get to Guardius in time. I am sorry. I am so sorry."

"Why are you here? I don't understand. You disappeared without a word. Why are you back?" Protectius furiously asked as he stood up.

Zaeem interrupted, "Protectius, now is not the time. I will need to take Guardius' body back to Magnetia. You need to go help the people in the Amphitheatre."

"Yes, yes. Jamilietta, do not disappear again. We need to talk," Protectius insisted.

"I have to go with Panacea right now, but I will return. I have much to tell you and someone I want to introduce you to," Jamilietta replied as she stood up and then said, "Panacea, there is nothing more you can do here, we must leave now."

Panacea slowly placed Guardius' head on the ground and stood up. Panacea and Jamilietta held hands and walked out of the stall.

Protectius scanned the stable and saw, in the corner of the stable, Sekhme's body lying on the ground.

Protectius looked at Zaeem and said, "That is Sekhme, Prince Yalem's wizardess. Guardius saved us all from her evil sorcery. May you rest in peace, my dear, dear friend."

Strongheart arrived with the Royal Carriage to King Zok's, aid and Prince Zaaki helped his parents and Star into the carriage. He then instructed the soldiers to head back to the palace without any further delay.

"Let the Royal Physician take a look at Father's wound as soon as you arrive," Prince Zaaki directed his order to Star, who agreed.

"Please be safe, my dear son," Queen Tee-Tee murmured. Prince Zaaki gave his mother a comforting nod before ordering the soldiers to leave. As the carriage departed in the direction of the palace, Star leaned out of the carriage window and waved at Prince Zaaki. Subsequently, Prince Zaaki mounted Strongheart, and they returned to the Royal Amphitheatre.

The Goddesses, with Karena, appeared in the entrance of one of the empty tunnels under the Amphitheatre that led to the stage. Goddess Ella and Goddess Lulu proceeded to telepathically summon Fred, Baal, Immanuel, Panacea and Jamilietta. Within a few minutes, Panacea and Jamilietta transported to the Goddesses, shortly followed by Fred and Immanuel. They waited for a few more minutes and Baal appeared floating through the tunnel on a dark grey cloud.

"We have done all that we can here, and we must return to the TransM School immediately. Jamilietta, I am aware of your unfinished business, and you will return soon. Panacea, unfortunately, it was Guardius' time. You were meant to save Zaeem, which you did." And with

Goddess Ella's words, they all vanished.

The Goddesses transported them all safely back to the TransM School.

Strongheart landed on the stage of the Royal Amphitheatre, and Prince Zaaki dismounted quickly as he saw the judges hiding in one of the tunnels under the tiered seating of the Amphitheatre.

"Are you all ok? Is anyone injured or hurt?" questioned a concerned Prince Zaaki.

"We are all fine. If we do not hold the ceremony today and proclaim you the winner, then the other Kingdoms will ask for a rematch," Aadeh explained, nervously.

"Very well, the ceremony will go ahead. We need the spectators to settle down," Prince Zaaki responded as he looked around the Amphitheatre at the scared faces of the people in the audience.

Prince Zaaki saw Protectius amongst the crowd and made his way to him.

"Protectius!" ordered Prince Zaaki, "The ceremony must go ahead. We need everyone to calm down and take their seats. Please tell the spectators they are safe now and they are not in any immediate danger."

Protectius looked at the Luellan soldiers and shouted, "Get everyone back in their seats. Inform them that they are safe now and to return to their seats."

Protectius and his army of soldiers rallied around the spectators, reassuring them that they were out of harm's way.

The spectators apprehensively resumed their places as Aadeh made an announcement, "The award ceremony is about to commence."

Aadeh looked up at the Royal Balcony and panicked as it was deserted. It was the role of the King of the land where the Battle of the Kingdoms takes place, to award the trophy and the co-ordinates of the new-found island to the winner of the battle.

Protectius accompanied Prince Zaaki to the stage, and all five judges walked onto the stage of the Royal Amphitheatre. There was a moment of silence and awkwardness before the Luellan band came out and marched in a circular pattern around the entire stage as they played a joyful and uplifting piece of music. Protectius stood on the sidelines and vigilantly watched every person who came close to Prince Zaaki.

The band stopped marching as they took their places, standing one meter apart encircling the outskirts of the stage. The piece of music they played ended, and suddenly, a display of fireworks erupted over the Royal Amphitheatre, lighting up the early evening sky.

In amazement, Prince Zaaki noticed King Zok, Queen Tee-Tee and Star walking onto the Royal Balcony and taking their seats once more.

He rushed to Protectius, "Why are they back here?"

Protectius looked up and saw them in the balcony, but before he could do anything, Aadeh initiated the award ceremony.

Aadeh addressed the people in the audience and the contestants and thanked them for their attendance. He continued to give a speech on the importance of the Battle of the Kingdoms and finally acknowledged the host Kingdom for their hospitality, despite the attack. He glanced at the Royal Balcony and was happily surprised to see the King and Queen back in their seats. He proceeded to ask King Zok to join him on the stage.

The drumroll commenced and King Zok announced the winner of the Battle of the Kingdoms. Aadeh handed King Zok the Battle of the Kingdoms trophy, which King Zok subsequently awarded to Prince Zaaki. The spectators all jumped from their seats to cheer and applaud. Star and Queen Tee-Tee stood up and loudly cheered for Prince Zaaki. He held the trophy above his head with delight as the sky lit up with fireworks for the finale of the Battle of the Kingdoms.

Goddess Lulu returned to the Royal Amphitheatre as Prince Zaaki was leaving to head back to the Royal Palace.

"Goddess Lulu, why have you returned?" Prince Zaaki curiously asked.

"I cannot rest until General Scarytis is taken to the cave prison where Vamwolf can keep a close eye on him. Will you accompany me?" requested Goddess Lulu, anxious to deal with this matter.

"Of course. Strongheart and myself will follow you and the General to Vamwolf," Prince Zaaki replied.

chapter Seventeen
XVII

The granite-grey sky faded as the sun awoke from its sleep. Total darkness turned into daylight as the sun's rays shone down on the picturesque Kingdom of Luella, as if nothing had changed. An array of fluffy white magic filled the sky, unsuccessfully trying to hide the bright sun and set the mood for the day forthwith.

The Magnetians were mourning the death of one of their great men, Guardius. It was the morning of his funeral and people from all over the Kingdom were arriving to pay their respects. Blizzardis and the Snowites arrived first, followed by Goldy and the Sizzlites.

Zaeem warmly greeted Blizzardis and Goldy and invited them into his home.

"Goldy, King Zok has ordered us to halt the work on the energy pipeline to the Kingdom of Yistyyim until he talks with their king. He has sent an invitation to King Salam to visit him and is awaiting his response," Zaeem informed her as he sat down on the couch in his living room.

Goldy nodded her head in acknowledgement to his instruction and wholeheartedly said, "I will notify the Sizzlites and tell them to return to Sizzi Village. I also wanted to convey my deepest condolences regarding Guardius. I did not know him well, but from what I have heard of him, he was a faithful and great Magnetian and soldier. If there is anything I can do, please let me know. The Sizzlites and myself are at your disposal and by your side. We are all Luellans and need to always be united."

Zaeem was sincerely moved by Goldy's words and responded, "Goldy, I appreciate you being here today and appreciate the kindness of you and the Sizzlites. The Magnetians and myself are also standing by your side if you should ever need us."

Blizzardis, in kind, added, "My deepest condolences from the Snowites and myself. We are also in union with the Magnetians and the Sizzlites to protect our great Kingdom."

Zaeem thanked Blizzardis and apprised him of Prince Zaaki's plan. "Blizzardis, firstly, thank you for your presence and support today, and thank you for the compassion of both you and the Snowites. Secondly, Prince Zaaki will be here shortly to inform you of his plan in the event of an attack from the Kingdom of Yistyyim. He does not know how they will respond to the death of Prince Yalem. We have sent the Yistyyim army back to their kingdom with the bodies of Prince Yalem and Sekhme."

Blizzardis enthusiastically reacted, "The Snowites and myself are at Prince Zaaki's service."

Goldy fearlessly interrupted, "As are the Sizzlites and myself. We can and will help to protect the Kingdom of Luella and the seas surrounding it."

Zaeem was pleased to hear that both the Sizzlites and Snowites would unite with the Magnetians and the Luellan army to protect their great Kingdom and the Royal Family. He portrayed his gratitude to them both as they awaited the imminent arrival of Prince Zaaki.

There was a knock at the door and Rosa, Zaeem's wife, went to answer it. Zaeem and Rosa's children, Bobby and Ginger, closely followed Rosa. She welcomed in Protectius and Prince Zaaki. As a sign of respect, Protectius and Prince Zaaki wore black suits with long black boots. Protectius hugged Rosa, and a wave of emotion came over him as he sobbed on her shoulder.

"Oh, Protectius. It is good to cry and be sad. It is a sad day for all of us. He was a good man and he admired you so much. Treasure the memories of him. We were all lucky enough to have him in our lives, albeit not for long," Rosa comforted Protectius.

Bobby and Ginger, overwrought with emotions, hugged Protectius and Prince Zaaki.

Protectius gathered himself, and Prince Zaaki patted him on his shoulder as Rosa showed them into the living room. Protectius shook Zaeem's hand, and they both looked at each other with tears in their eyes. Prince Zaaki greeted Goldy and Blizzardis and commiserated Zaeem on his loss before they all sat down. They all spoke of Guardius, and Zaeem shared his fondest memories of him. After a while, they discussed a possible attack from the Kingdom of Yistyyim and formulated a plan to defend the Kingdom of Luella from any such violence.

Rosa entered the living room and softly spoke, "We must make our way to the funeral now. We cannot keep everyone waiting."

"Zaeem, my parents are attending. Let us not keep them waiting," stated Prince Zaaki as they all stood up and exited Zaeem's house.

Rosa wiped a tear from her cheek and gathered herself together before making her way to the funeral with Bobby and Ginger. The kids both carried flowers they had picked themselves, ready to place them on Guardius' grave.

For the Magnetians, a funeral was a grand occasion, more so than a wedding. It was a ceremony to celebrate a person's life, all the while mourning the person's passing. It was a time of great sadness, but also a time of hope for what is to come next.

As Guardius' body lay in the mahogany closed casket, draped with the Kingdom of Luella's flag, a holy woman officiated the service and spoke of Guardius' great life. She spoke of his love, his kindness and his compassion for others and for life.

After which, the casket was slowly lowered into the grave, and Zaeem somberly said a few words. "Guardius, I will always remember and appreciate how protective you were of me and my family. You never ceased to surprise me with your compassion to protect Magnetia and our beloved Magnetians. You were always there when I needed you and when others needed help. You faced danger in the eye and fought it, to protect Magnetia and our great Kingdom. You will always be remembered as a bold, courageous, fearless and loyal man. We honour your life here today and send you on your way to a new beginning somewhere out there."

Zaeem picked up some mud and threw it onto the coffin. Protectius stepped forward and also threw some mud onto the coffin as he bid farewell to his loyal friend, followed by Prince Zaaki, who did the same.

King Zok advanced towards the grave, and as he threw some mud over his coffin, he said, "Guardius, we all commend you on your loyalty and love of our Kingdom. Thank you for your service. You will be greatly missed."

All the men, including Blizzardis, followed suit and threw mud on the grave.

Finally, Queen Tee-Tee approached the grave and threw a white flower on top of it, shortly followed by Star, who also gave her respects and threw a white flower into the grave. Goldy followed suit as she bid Guardius farewell.

Once everyone had paid their respects, they all stood by his grave in a moment of silence and solidarity before slowly departing the funeral.

Rosa stayed behind with Bobby and Ginger. The two placed the flowers they brought with them by his grave and said their goodbyes as they sobbed in their mother's arms.

After the funeral, Star and Prince Zaaki bid farewell to King Zok and Queen Tee-Tee as they boarded the Royal Carriage and returned to the Royal Palace.

Prince Zaaki took Star's hand without saying a word, and they went for a stroll in the purple fields, beyond where the funeral took place. They walked in a comforting silence until the sun slowly faded and the day turned into night. Star and Prince Zaaki reached the Pink Crystal Rocks that glistened under the moonlight and gazed at their wonder.

Prince Zaaki turned to face Star, took hold of her other hand and conveyed his feelings. "Star, I have been preoccupied of late with the affairs of the Kingdom and have not given you much attention. For this, I apologise. You deserve more, and of this I am capable. Unexpected incidents occur which are out of my hands and which I must deal with. I want to thank you for waiting patiently for me. The love we share cannot be denied. It is an overwhelming love I have for you, and I want to share my life with you. Your gift saved my life."

Prince Zaaki removed the compass from his pocket and showed Star. The compass had a dent in it, and he briefly retold her what happened. Star examined the compass to see a significant dent in it, which made her heart race with anxiety over Prince Zaaki's safety. Star longed for and prayed for Prince Zaaki's well-being and safety, for the love she had for him was immeasurable.

Star listened to every word and fervently declared her love, "Zaaki, I am wholly and unreservedly in love with you. I am relieved and extremely grateful for you and your safe return to me. I want to share my life with you, but I feel an urgency to tell you of my recent feelings. Since the day you defended the King and Queen and myself, and my father and sister died at your hands, it has tormented me. I cannot escape this horrid vision and I am torn between my love for you and the surprising love, which I did not know I had, for my own family. I have spoken to your mother of this, and she helped me to process it. Although I still feel that we need to speak of this."

Prince Zaaki's eyes fixated on hers as he replied, "I am truly sorry that they died at my hands. I was protecting you and my parents, and I will go to any lengths to protect you. But I do wish there was another way. It plays on my mind every day, and I try to think of different scenarios in which they were captured instead of being killed. I feel an immeasurable amount of guilt that it happened the way it did. But please know this: your family are people who care and love you Star, unconditionally and forever. And I vow to love you unconditionally and forever. I know that my mother is very fond of you and loves and cares for you. We are your family. It hurts me that you are hurting, and I wish I could erase this memory to ease your pain. Thank you for telling me; I want us to always be able to tell each other anything and never withhold secrets from one another." Prince Zaaki's eyes welled up. "Star, I never want to hurt you, and I am profusely apologetic that I did. Please forgive me, as I am unable to forgive myself."

Star's emotions intensified, and she wrapped her arms around Prince Zaaki. She felt a sense of relief that she communicated her feelings. Prince Zaaki tightly hugged her back for a few moments under the stars, repeatedly asking for her forgiveness.

Star consoled Prince Zaaki. "Zaaki, I love you and always will. You should have told me that these thoughts consume you as they have been consuming me. Of course, I forgive you. You did what you had to do, and knowing that you feel remorse helps me to see that you do love me. Knowing that you wish it could have resulted with them being captured instead of being killed helps also. I know there was no other way, and you were protecting your family. So yes. Yes, I do forgive you. I love you with all my heart and always will."

Prince Zaaki wiped away his tears, pulled away from the

embrace and knelt down on one knee. He removed a small crimson box from his pocket, opened it and held it out.

"Your love and understanding never cease to amaze me. You make me want to be a better person every day. I am completely in love with you. And so, Star, under the stars of Luella, will you give me your hand in marriage?" Prince Zaaki reverently asked.

Star knelt down opposite him and said, "I would love nothing more. Yes!"

Star gave Prince Zaaki another warm embrace before he placed the beautiful emerald diamond ring on her finger.

"We had better make our way back to the village and get Strongheart to fly us home," an ecstatic Prince Zaaki suggested as he helped Star up.

Protectius sat on a bench on the front porch of his house and reminisced of times he shared with Guardius. They were the best of friends and taught each other how to duel. As Protectius was getting up to go inside, Jamilietta appeared with Fred and gave Protectius a fright. He fell back down on the bench, staring at Jamilietta and Fred.

"Hello, Protectius, I want to introduce you to Fred,"

Jamilietta paused for a while to allow her and her son's presence to sink in before resuming. "He is our son."

Protectius was speechless and could not believe what he was hearing.

"I know this comes as a shock to you, but I hope you will listen to what I have to say. I was young and foolish, but mostly, I was scared, Protectius."

"Scared of what? I loved you, and I gave you everything. How could you leave me, knowing you were with child?" Protectius questioned, upset and confused.

"It was because I was with child that I left. I tried so many times to tell you of my powers, but I could not bring myself to say the words. I was scared that I would not be able to stop our child from using his powers in front of you and that it would frighten you. I was worried that you would leave us. Fred and I are different. I have come to appreciate and value my gift; it is not bad or evil in any way. We only use it to help people. I am sorry I hurt you and that you were not there for Fred's birth or since. I took that from you, and it aches deep in my heart that I did that. Protectius, I am so sorry." Jamilietta broke down in tears.

Protectius stood up and walked to Fred and looked at him. Instantly, Fred wrapped his little arms around his father and squeezed. Protectius hugged him back and then began to laugh.

"I have a son! I have a son!" Protectius hailed out loud.

Protectius invited Jamilietta and Fred inside, where he made them all some tea, and Protectius asked Fred to tell him about his life. They spoke into the early hours of the morning sharing stories and adventures of what they had experienced.

Prince Zaaki and Strongheart entered the Zenith Temple and made their way to the TransM room. Strongheart waited outside as Prince Zaaki entered. The Goddesses, Charon and Karena were awaiting his presence to commence.

"Thank you for attending the transmigration of Guardius' soul. Karena and Charon, you may start," Goddess Lulu graciously verbalized.

Prince Zaaki watched in awe of this supernatural phenomenon taking place before his very eyes. Utterly captivated by Charon and Karena's gift of helping souls pass from one life to another, tears fell from his eyes and strolled down his cheeks. He was overcome with a feeling of elation that Guardius' soul was about to start another journey. As he watched this exquisite and majestical ceremony take place, Prince Zaaki hoped that one day they might meet again.

chapter Eighteen
XVIII

A month had passed since the Battle of the Kingdoms, and King Zok had not heard from the King of Yistyyim, so he assumed that the King was too ashamed of his son's actions to respond. With this, King Zok and Queen Tee-Tee agreed that the engagement event for Prince Zaaki and Star could take place. King Zok sent for Protectius, who had taken time off to spend with his wife and son.

Queen Tee-Tee summoned Prince Zaaki and Star to join her on the floating silver cloud-like balcony in the grand living room of the Royal Palace. Queen Tee-Tee sipped her tea as she gazed into the picturesque Royal Gardens of the palace from the resplendent windows opposite her. The sunlight reflected off the bright green and yellow windows, and the colours reflected throughout the living room, bringing it to life. Peacefully munching on some golden berries hanging on the tall exotic trees that lined the gardens, were the Girtigs in all their wondrous glory. The red Catbirds were making beautiful music as they flew around the gardens, whilst the striped blue-and-gold Zebflas were chasing each other in a light-hearted game of catch. Queen Tee-Tee appreciated the magnificent splendor that engulfed her.

Queen Tee-Tee, wanting to hear the music of the Catbirds more clearly, asked one of the guards on duty to open all the oval-shaped grand windows in the living room. Once all the windows were opened, a gentle breeze with the exquisite aroma of the multi-coloured flowers made its way into the living room and invaded it with the most alluring scent.

Prince Zaaki held onto Star's waist with one hand as he hovered them both to the floating balcony. They both stepped off the hoverboard onto the floating balcony and proceeded to greet the Queen before sitting down.

"You have had a month to quietly enjoy your engagement before announcing it to the Kingdom of Luella. I do not mean to meddle in your affairs, but it is time. The King and I have discussed it at length, and it is time for the engagement event to go ahead. You requested that we give you space to enjoy being together without prying eyes, and with respect, we have granted you that. Now you must endeavour to attend the party that I will hold in your honour ten days from today, hence you have a few more days to spend as you wish," Queen Tee-Tee respectfully informed Prince Zaaki and Star as she poured them tea.

"We appreciate that you have respected our privacy over the course of the past month, and we understand that the time has come to announce our engagement. I will be leaving tomorrow to go visit the new island and place the flag of the Kingdom of Luella on its highest point. Aadeh is pushing me to name the island, thus I feel it imperative I see it before naming it. I will be back in two days," said Prince Zaaki, addressing both his mother and Star.

"Very good, my dear son. That will give Star and I ample time to start preparations for the engagement event," Queen Tee-Tee happily remarked.

"I will be happy to help, Your Majesty," Star tenderly voiced.

"Help? You will not be just helping, my dear Star, this special evening is your engagement. You will be telling me what you want, and you will oversee everything, from the hors d'oeuvres and guests to the flower arrangements and entertainment. I will be helping you, my dear child. This is your night. This is the start of your lives together, and I want it to be exactly as you envisioned," Queen Tee-Tee insisted as she held Star's hand over the table that separated them.

"Your Majesty, I am tremendously grateful for your support, generosity and love. Thank you for all you have done for me," Star expressed her gratitude for the Queen's kindness.

"That is settled. Do you require anything else from us?" Prince Zaaki asked his mother as he sipped his tea.

"That is all, my dears. You may leave," declared Queen

Tee-Tee, dismissing them.

Strongheart, with Prince Zaaki on his back departed the Royal Palace at sunrise and headed towards the co-ordinates of the new island. They followed the River Tara until they reached the sublime mountains of the Kingdom of Luella. They flew over the Great Snow Blue Mountain towards the Souls Sea without stopping. Prince Zaaki and Strongheart enjoyed the majestic beauty the Kingdom of Luella offered from this height. The sun was lying down to sleep as they neared Sizzi Village in the Souls Sea.

Prince Zaaki ordered Strongheart to fly to Pos Island so they could rest at the TransM School for the night, then continue their journey to the new island in the morning.

Goddess Lulu and Goddess Ella welcomed Prince Zaaki and Strongheart into the Zenith Temple, and they showed Strongheart to the indoor stables to rest for the night. The Goddesses proceeded to show Prince Zaaki to his suite for the night.

"Goddess Lulu, Goddess Ella, everything you have shown me thus far has consumed my mind and soul. I want to learn more. I am ready for more. It is enchanting in a most blessed way to begin to understand our purpose here. I did not realise how sacred the soul of every being is. You have opened my eyes to such amazement, and I appreciate my life and the life of every person so much more, tremendously more. Knowledge is the key, and I want to learn," Prince Zaaki proclaimed.

"Prince Zaaki, all in due time. Soon, you will be visiting us more regularly, and you will learn more of the truths of life. Please remember, you are learning with every breath you take and every adventure you encounter. You are learning with every new person that enters your life. You are learning when you look around and appreciate nature and all the wildlife. You are learning when you have respect for the Kingdom you live in and all the other Kingdoms in the realm. Keep your eyes wide open and take it all in. As long as you are eager to learn, you will become more knowledgeable of all that is around you and inside you," Goddess Ella elegantly explained.

"Sleep well, Prince Zaaki. We shall see you for breakfast before you make your way to the new island," Goddess Lulu commented as she gracefully floated away on her cloud, closely followed by Goddess Ella.

Strongheart and Prince Zaaki landed on the new island, in a forest high up on a mountain. The mountainous island was covered with a sea of cedar trees as far as the eye could see. The tops of the mountains were blanketed with clouds, and the cedar trees looked as if they were trying to reach the heavens; not just trying, but succeeding. Prince Zaaki and Strongheart could clearly hear the soft breeze whistling through the leaves and branches of the cedars.

"What greatness lies here, Strongheart. Nature in all its glory. Take it all in," Prince Zaaki whispered as he took in a deep breath of fresh mountain air.

The mountains were draped with the intense incense of the astoundingly great cedars. All of Prince Zaaki's senses were heightened as he captured the wondrous beauty of this island. In awe of this island and in complete silence, Prince Zaaki and Strongheart explored the island on foot. Happiness and contentment filled their bodies as they could feel and hear the magnificent cedars breathe. They could smell their perfume, and as they touched their old and wise bark, Prince Zaaki and Strongheart were overcome with elation.

The cedars grew side-by-side and grew to enormous height and width, protecting the land, which was carpeted with the most beautiful purple grass, from the four seasons. They hiked to the top of one of the mountains and stood by a cedar tree engulfed in the clouds. Prince Zaaki, amazed by all this untouched nature, decided then and there that this island was a sacred place and that it should not be disturbed by man.

"Strongheart, I feel like I'm in a dream. These cedars are breathtaking." Prince Zaaki took a short pause and announced his decision, "I shall name this island, The Alarez Luella Island."

Prince Zaaki removed the flag of the Kingdom of Luella from the bag on Strongheart's back and planted its wooden base in the soil by the cedar tree. The flag stood erect and swayed back and forth in the direction of the subtle breeze as the leaves of the cedars made majestical music.

"That is a marvellous name, Prince Zaaki. I've never seen such beauty, in all my years. I wish we could stay for longer, but we really should be getting back to the palace now. If we are not to stop on the way, we should make it by nightfall," suggested Strongheart.

Prince Zaaki gazed across the magnificent island for a few more moments before mounting Strongheart and heading back to the Royal Palace in the Kingdom of Luella.

It was the eve of Prince Zaaki and Star's engagement celebration, and guests were arriving from all over the Kingdom. Star had decided to call the event, "The Blue Snow Ball." She wanted to turn the Royal Palace into a blue wonderland of snow with amusements in the Royal Gardens and the grand ballroom of the Royal Palace. Star had read about and heard stories from Prince Zaaki about the Great Snow Blue Mountain and yearned to visit it one day. But until that day, she wanted to re-create her own vision of what it looked like and share it with her honoured guests.

Blizzardis and Goldy were involved in the preparations

for The Blue Snow Ball and helped Star and Queen Tee-Tee create a magical and mesmerizing event. Blizzardis employed a hundred Snowites to run the amusements set up in the gardens of the palace while Goldy employed a hundred Sizzlites to tend to the guests in the grand ballroom and dining room of the palace. Zaeem was still in mourning over his friend and confidante, Guardius, hence he was invited as a guest to enjoy the evening with his wife, Rosa.

Protectius organised the Luellan army to secure the grounds and stand guard at all entrances and exits. Futuris created man-made blue snow to cover the entire grounds of the palace and a light blue fog that swept over the snow. Amongst the elaborate ice sculptures that circled the Royal Gardens, one in particular stood out the most. It was a detailed sculpture of Guardius, shining coldly in the evening light. It sat as the centerpiece of the main garden, where everyone could see it in all its glory.

Guests were welcomed with mystifying puffs of blue and pink smoke fluttering over the drinks, infused with orange blossom and rose water. Orange blossom being Prince Zaaki's favourite drink, and rose water being Star's favourite.

Protectius arrived with Jamilietta on his arm, looking the happiest he had ever been.

Once all the guests had arrived, they were all invited into the grand ballroom. Music and laughter resonated throughout the grand ballroom. All of a sudden, the music halted, and the guests went quiet as they looked to the extravagant doors of the grand ballroom. A single trumpet launched into the Kingdom of Luella's national anthem, and the doors opened. King Zok entered with Queen Tee-Tee by his side, and the guests took a few steps back to make a path for the King and Queen to enter the ballroom and take their seats on their thrones.

Prince Zaaki, hair slicked back tidily, wearing a dark green suit, the sleeves laced in the most exquisite diamonds, walked in behind his parents, holding hands with Star. Star wore a long sleeveless silver gown with a long tail encrusted with heart shaped diamonds. They both took their places, adjacent to King Zok and Queen Tee-Tee.

King Zok stood up from his throne and announced, "Welcome, everyone! Thank you for coming and sharing this wonderful evening with us. I am pleased to formally announce the engagement of my son, Prince Zaaki and Star. Join Queen Tee-Tee and I in wishing the happy couple congratulations."

All the guests applauded Prince Zaaki and Star, and that was the cue for Brunelli Marsi. The singer started singing a song he had written especially for the newly engaged couple, accompanied by the grand Royal Orchestra of Luella. Star had organised this singer and aided Brunelli in writing this song as a gift to her betrothed on their very special evening.

Some guests started to dance to the music, whilst others made their way to the Royal Gardens where Snowites put on shows in various parts of the gardens.

Prince Zaaki held out his hand to Star and asked her to dance, and she graciously accepted. They danced throughout the course of most of the evening, enthralled in each other's eyes, oblivious to everyone around them.

Protectius and Jamilietta joined Prince Zaaki and Star on the dance floor. Zaeem and Rosa followed suit, and they all danced close to each other. Protectius tapped Prince Zaaki on the shoulder and congratulated him and Star.

"Thank you. You look happy, Protectius. Actually, I have never seen you quite this happy before. It suits you," Prince Zaaki cheered.

They all continued to dance to Vivaldi, their feet majestically swaying through the blue snow and mist. The Royal Ballroom was decorated with blue and white flowers and heart-shaped ice sculptures. The blue floating cloud-like balconies were decorated with large blue crystals and the Sizzlites were standing by to escort guests up to the balconies on the hoverboards.

Star whispered in Prince Zaaki's ear, "Zaaki, can we go for a walk through the gardens now? I want to show you something. I think Zaeem and Protectius would appreciate it as well. They can join us if you wish."

Prince Zaaki nodded in agreement and invited Protectius, Jamilietta, Zaeem and Rosa to accompany him and Star on a stroll around the gardens of the palace. Star took them through the gardens to the main garden where they were all stunned to see the masterpiece in the center surrounded by blue mystical fog. It was the life-sized ice sculpture of Guardius.

"I hope you all like it. I asked Futuris to do this so that it would feel as if he were here with us to celebrate our engagement," spoke Star hesitantly.

Prince Zaaki placed his arm around Star's shoulder as his eyes remained focused on the ice sculpture and replied, "It's perfect. Thank you."

Zaeem and Protectius concurred with Prince Zaaki and thanked Star for this thoughtful piece of art.

"I think Jamilietta and I will continue to look around at the splendid shows the Snowites are performing," Protectius stated as he walked off hand-in-hand with Jamilietta.

Rosa linked arms with Zaeem and gave him a look. Zaeem knew that look and excused himself and Rosa.

Prince Zaaki held Star's hand, and they made their way back into the ballroom for one final dance to end their perfect evening.

King Zok retired to his suite for the night after a beautiful engagement for his son and Star. He was happily humming to one of the songs played that evening as he closed the door of his room and sat on the edge of his bed. A joyous King Zok was happy and content that his son had found the love of his life and was engaged to her. He saw a kindness in Star that eased his mind over his son's future as King. King Zok acknowledged that he could not have been a successful king without the support and love of his wife. She was his rock through all the challenges he faced, and through all the good times, she kept him grounded and humble. King Zok felt overtly proud of Prince Zaaki and was delighted to show him off to all their guests this evening.

He leaned down, smiling as he reminisced the evening's events, to remove his boots, and as he sat back up, a flicker of motion caught his eye. He began to turn, but a masked man leapt out from behind the large curtains, a dagger glinting in the dim light. King Zok's grin turned into a frown of disbelief and shock. The assassin drove the dagger into King Zok's chest, piercing his heart. Gasping, King Zok slid off his bed and collapsed onto the ground. He feebly pawed at the dagger, his hands shaking. The assassin removed a large piece of cloth from his pocket and unfolded it. Subsequently, he draped it over King Zok's body and fled out of the window. King Zok, unable to voice any words, lay on the floor of his room, covered by the flag of the Kingdom of Yistyyim, bleeding out.

THE END

Heba Hamzeh

Heba Hamzeh is well known for creating and writing *Prince Zaaki and The Royal Sword of Luella*. Heba is a mother of three extraordinary children and it was them that inspired her to create Prince Zaaki and all the incredible characters and magical places within her books. *Prince Zaaki and The Momentous Battle of The Kingdoms* is the second book in the Prince Zaaki series, where new places and new characters are introduced and explored. Heba has enjoyed evolving the main characters from the first book and developing the storyline. During her time spent writing this book, Heba has already planned and set about writing the third book in the Prince Zaaki series.

A note from the author: I hope you, the readers, enjoy this book as much as I did writing it and telling it to my children.

To follow the author:

@hebahamzehauthor

@hebahauthor